BILLY BATSON AND THE MAGIC OF SHAZAM!

STONE ARCH BOOKS
a capstone imprint

STONE ARCH BOOKS™

Published in 2015 by Stone Arch Books
A Capstone Imprint
1710 Roe Crest Drive
North Mankato, MN 56003
www.capstonepub.com

Originally published by DC Comics in the U.S.
in single magazine form as Billy Batson and
the Magic of SHAZAM! #5.
Copyright © 2015 DC Comics. All Rights Reserved.

DC COMICS

1700 Broadway, New York, NY 10019
A Warner Bros. Entertainment Company
No part of this publication may be reproduced in
whole or in part, or stored in a retrieval system, or
transmitted in any form or by any means, electronic,
mechanical, photocopying, recording, or otherwise,
without written permission.
Printed in China by Nordica.
0914/CA21401510
092014   008470NORDS15

Cataloging-in-Publication Data is available at the Library
of Congress website.
ISBN: 978-1-4342-9656-6 (library binding)

Summary: With the help of two sentient cockroaches,
the villain Dr. Sivana has recently escaped from Fawcett
City Penitentiary. The mad scientist unleashes robotic
mayhem on the city of Fawcett, but he needs more
power to finish his hostile takeover . . . and it seems
that Captain Marvel and Mary Marvel might be just
what the doctor ordered!

STONE ARCH BOOKS

Ashley C. Andersen Zantop **Publisher**
Michael Dahl **Editorial Director**
Sean Tulien **Editor**
Heather Kindseth **Creative Director**
Kristi Carlson and Peggie Carley **Designers**

DC COMICS

Dan Didio **Original U.S. Editor**

BILLY BATSON
AND THE MAGIC OF
SHAZAM!

Mr. Who?
Mr. Atom!

Art Baltazar & Franco ....writers
Byron Vaughns...............................penciller
Ken Branch... inker
Dave Tanguay................................ colorist

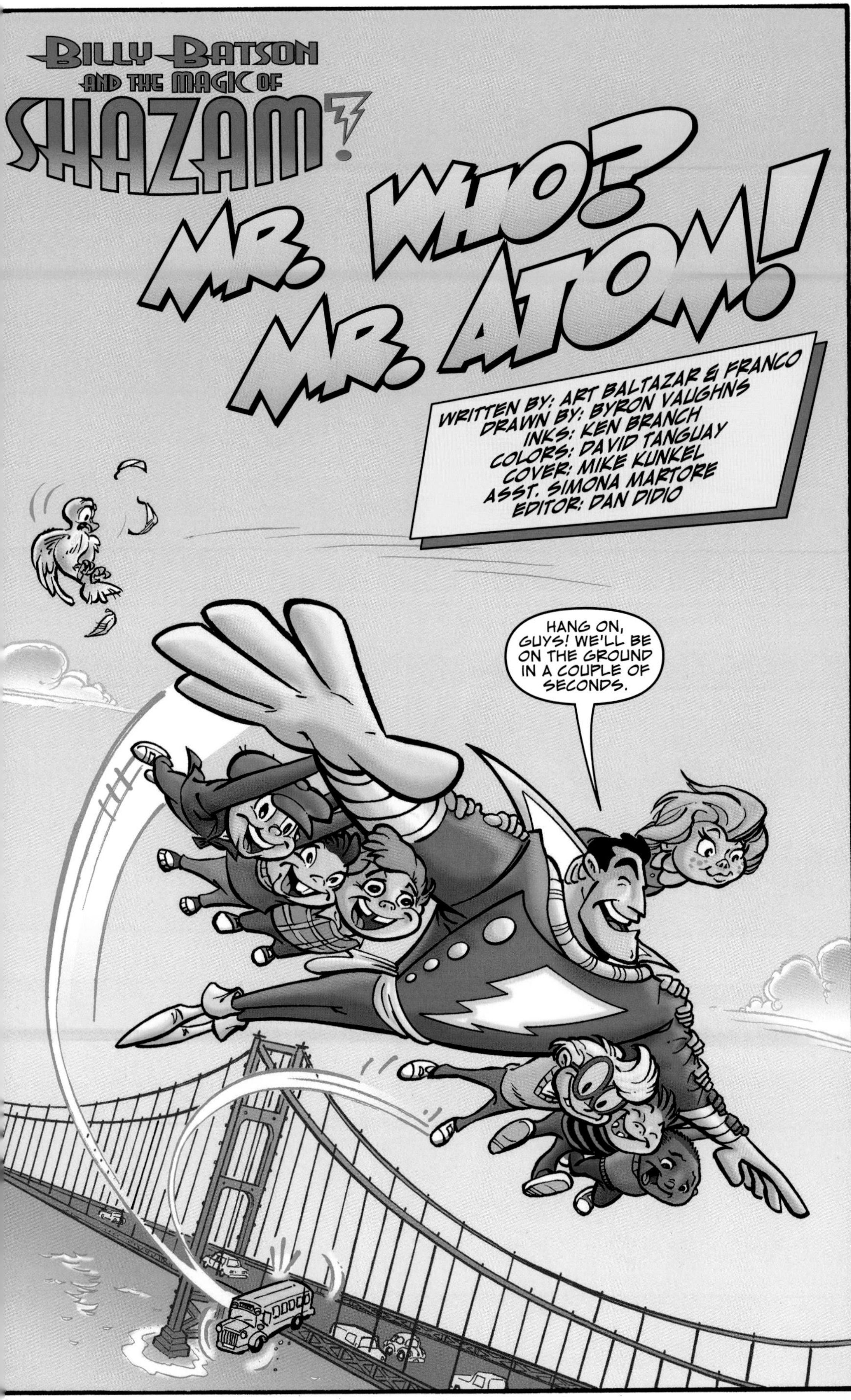
BILLY BATSON AND THE MAGIC OF SHAZAM!
MR. WHO? MR. ATOM!
WRITTEN BY: ART BALTAZAR & FRANCO
DRAWN BY: BYRON VAUGHNS
INKS: KEN BRANCH
COLORS: DAVID TANGUAY
COVER: MIKE KUNKEL
ASST. SIMONA MARTORE
EDITOR: DAN DIDIO
HANG ON, GUYS! WE'LL BE ON THE GROUND IN A COUPLE OF SECONDS.

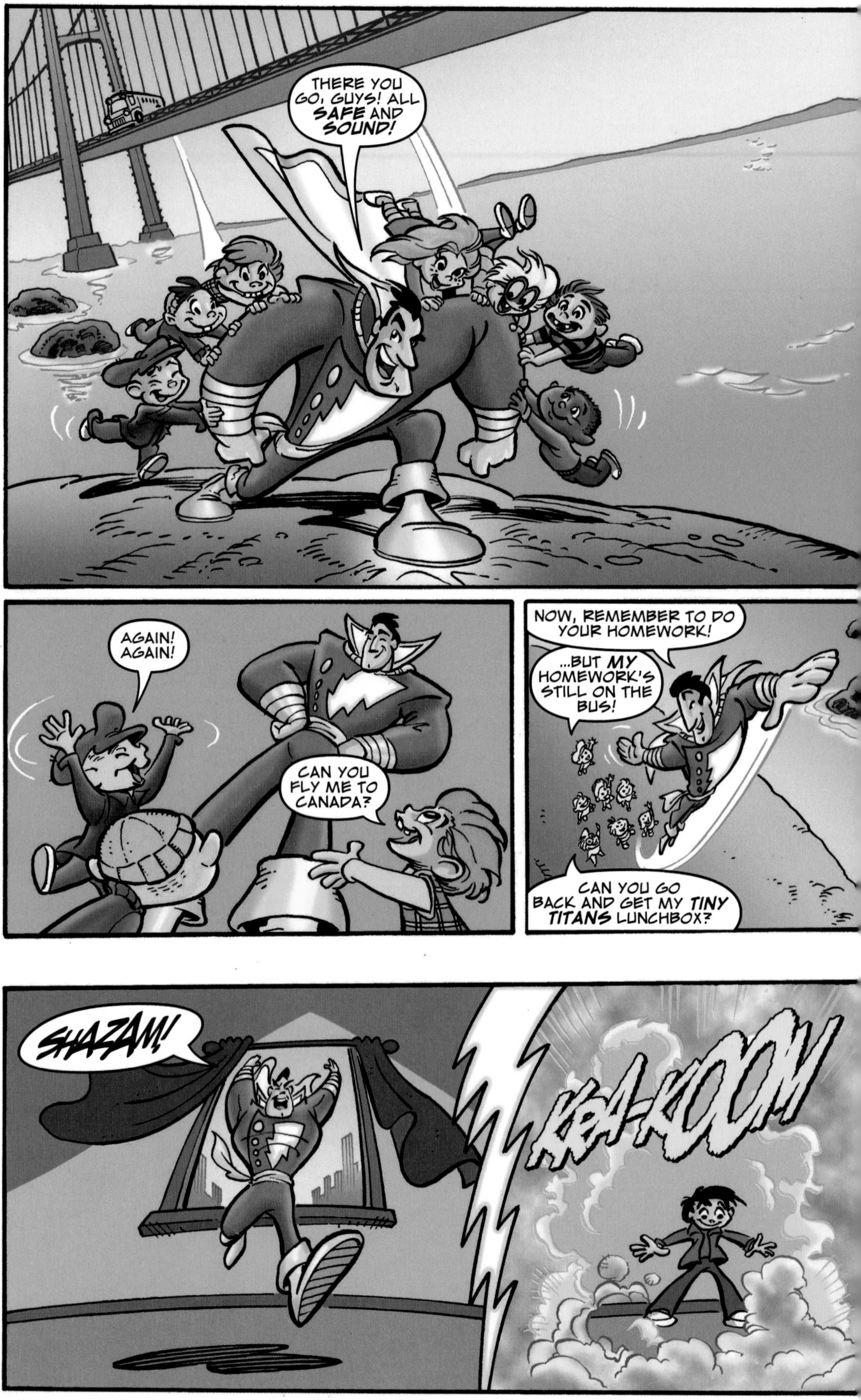

THERE YOU GO, GUYS! ALL SAFE AND SOUND!
AGAIN! AGAIN!
CAN YOU FLY ME TO CANADA?
NOW, REMEMBER TO DO YOUR HOMEWORK!
...BUT MY HOMEWORK'S STILL ON THE BUS!
CAN YOU GO BACK AND GET MY TINY TITANS LUNCHBOX?
SHAZAM!
KRA-KOOM

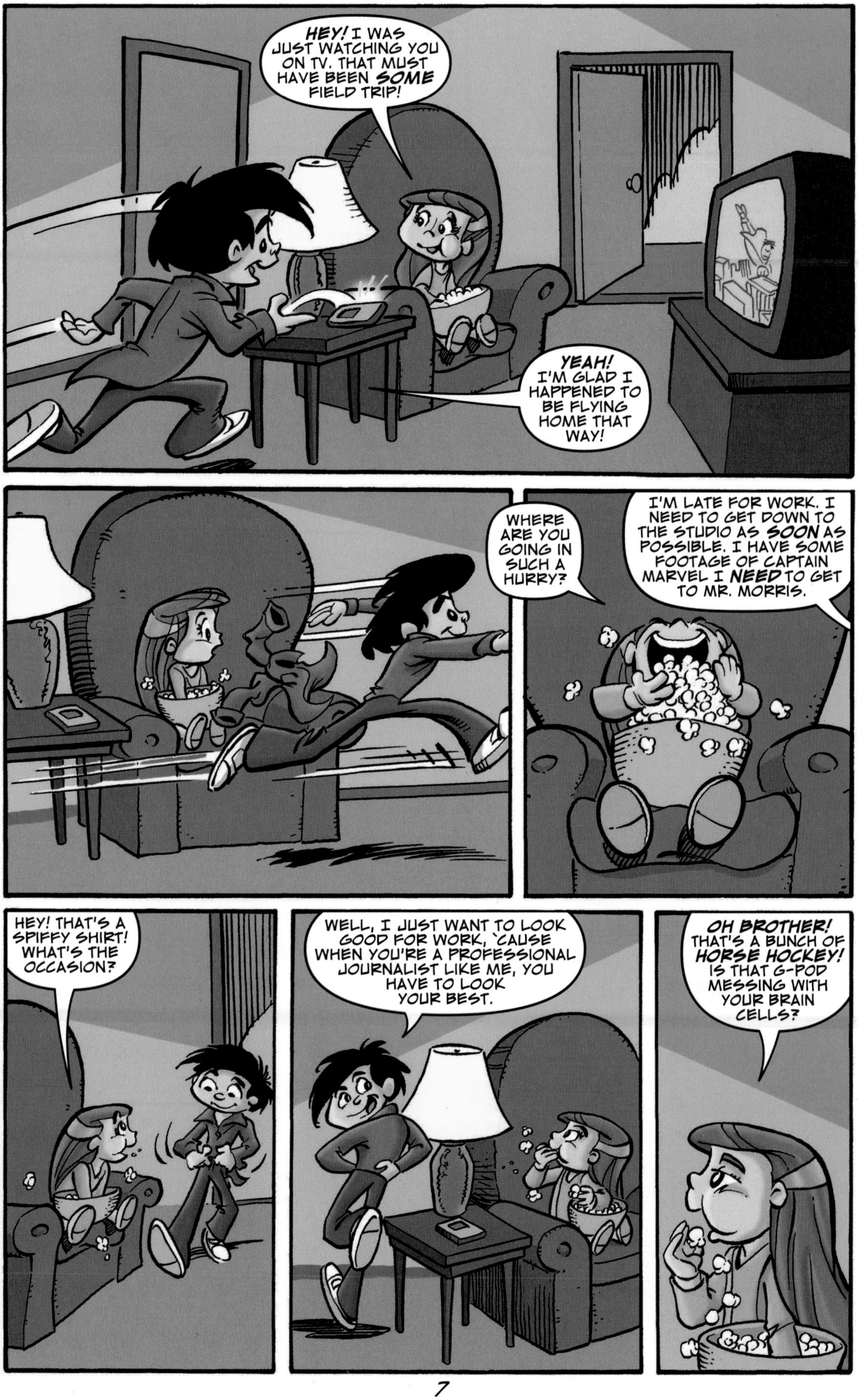
HEY! I WAS JUST WATCHING YOU ON TV. THAT MUST HAVE BEEN SOME FIELD TRIP!
YEAH! I'M GLAD I HAPPENED TO BE FLYING HOME THAT WAY!
WHERE ARE YOU GOING IN SUCH A HURRY?
I'M LATE FOR WORK. I NEED TO GET DOWN TO THE STUDIO AS SOON AS POSSIBLE. I HAVE SOME FOOTAGE OF CAPTAIN MARVEL I NEED TO GET TO MR. MORRIS.
HEY! THAT'S A SPIFFY SHIRT! WHAT'S THE OCCASION?
WELL, I JUST WANT TO LOOK GOOD FOR WORK, `CAUSE WHEN YOU'RE A PROFESSIONAL JOURNALIST LIKE ME, YOU HAVE TO LOOK YOUR BEST.
OH BROTHER! THAT'S A BUNCH OF HORSE HOCKEY! IS THAT G-POD MESSING WITH YOUR BRAIN CELLS?

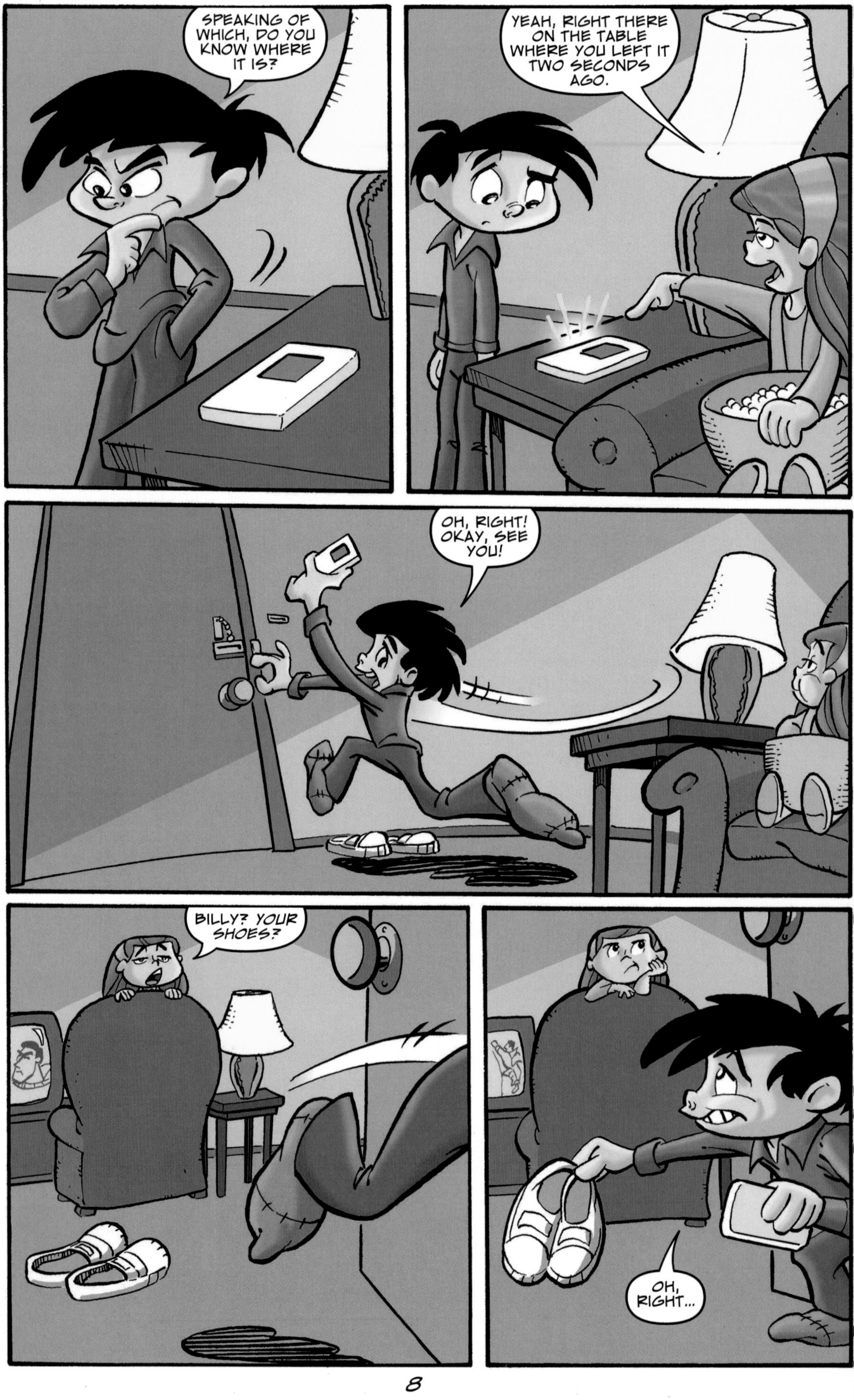
SPEAKING OF WHICH, DO YOU KNOW WHERE IT IS?
YEAH, RIGHT THERE ON THE TABLE WHERE YOU LEFT IT TWO SECONDS AGO.
OH, RIGHT! OKAY, SEE YOU!
BILLY? YOUR SHOES?
OH, RIGHT...

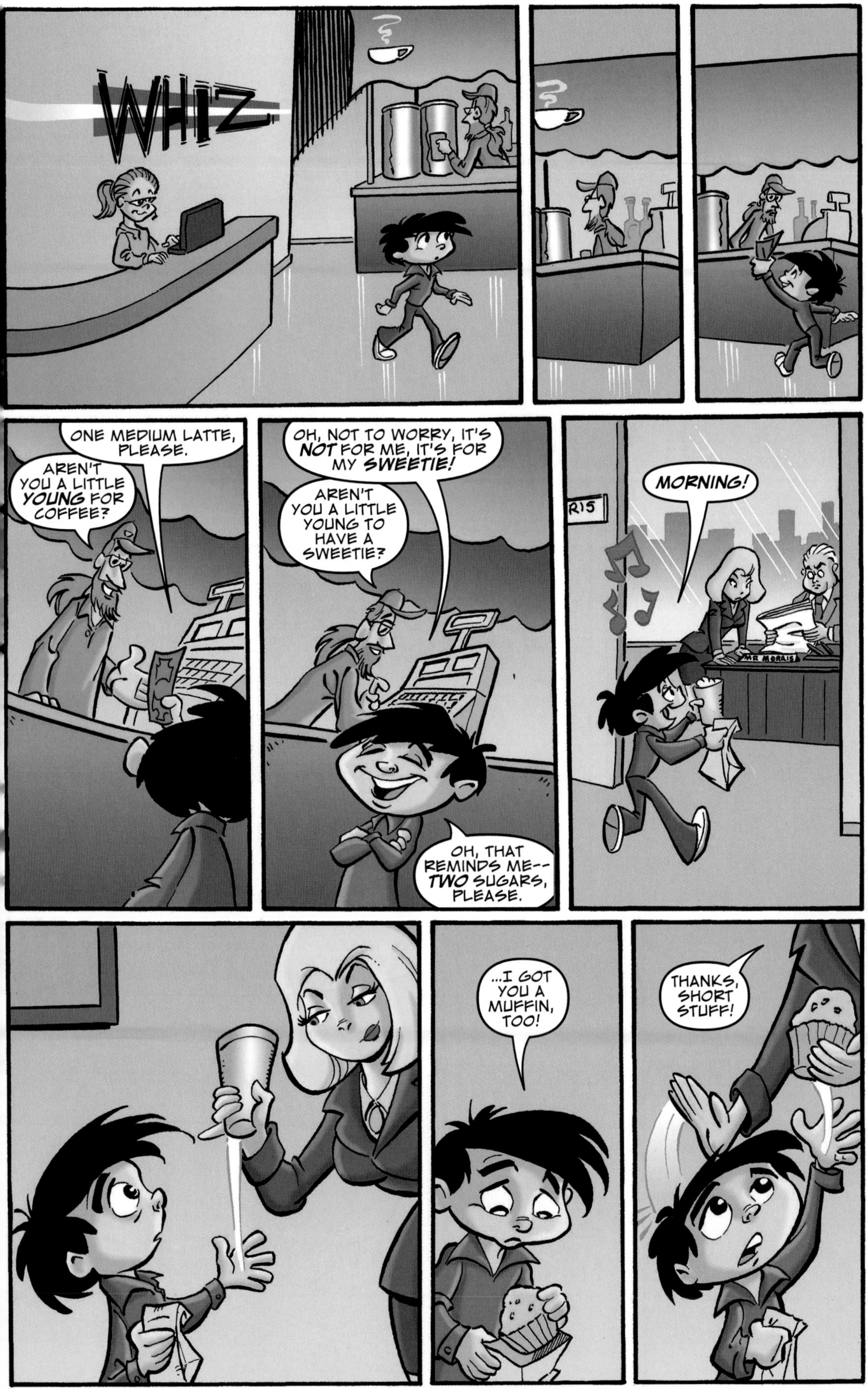
WHIZ
ONE MEDIUM LATTE, PLEASE.
AREN'T YOU A LITTLE YOUNG FOR COFFEE?
OH, NOT TO WORRY, IT'S NOT FOR ME, IT'S FOR MY SWEETIE!
AREN'T YOU A LITTLE YOUNG TO HAVE A SWEETIE?
OH, THAT REMINDS ME-- TWO SUGARS, PLEASE.
RIS
MORNING!
MR MORRIS
...I GOT YOU A MUFFIN, TOO!
THANKS, SHORT STUFF!

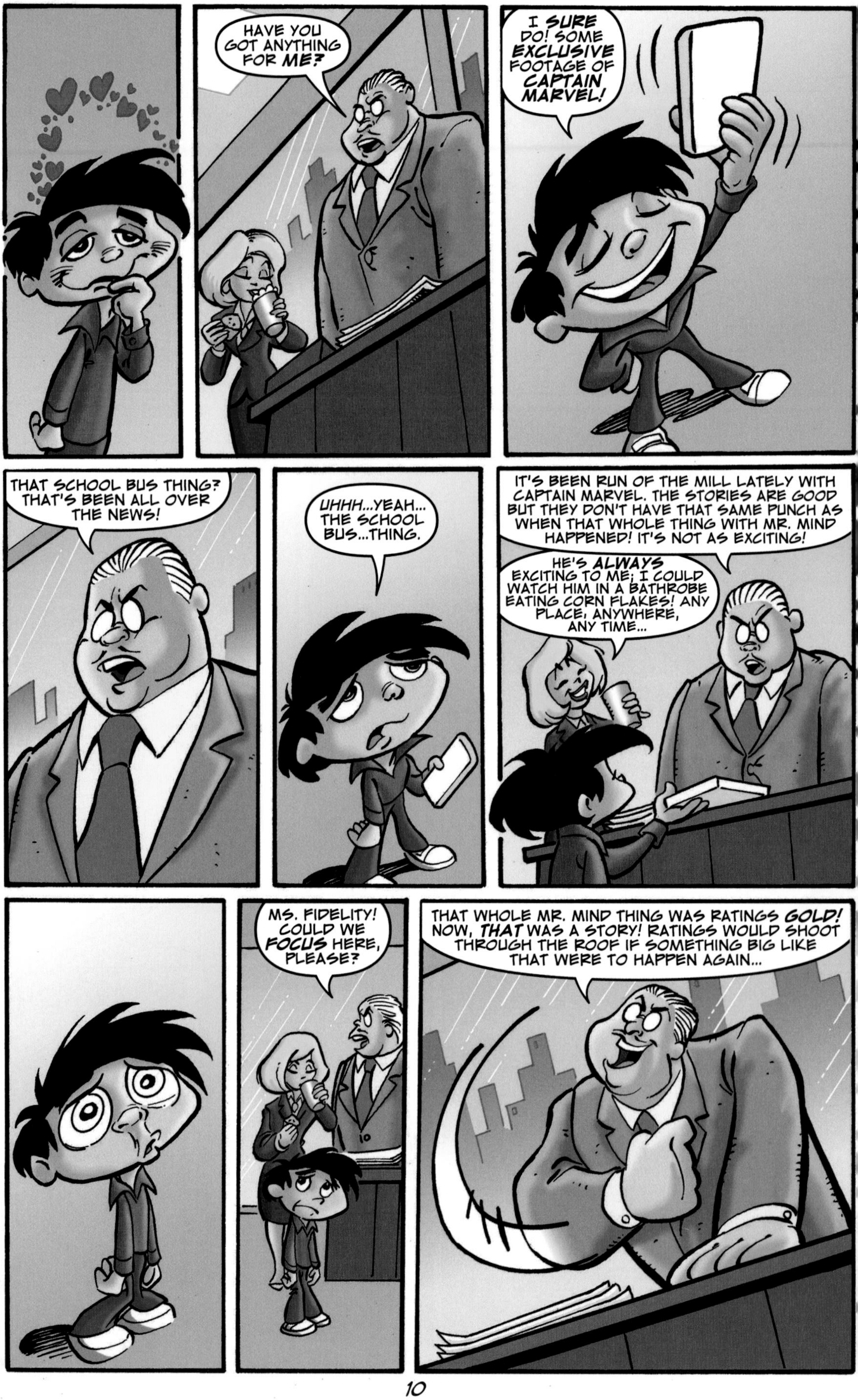
HAVE YOU GOT ANYTHING FOR ME?
I SURE DO! SOME EXCLUSIVE FOOTAGE OF CAPTAIN MARVEL!
THAT SCHOOL BUS THING? THAT'S BEEN ALL OVER THE NEWS!
UHHH...YEAH... THE SCHOOL BUS...THING.
IT'S BEEN RUN OF THE MILL LATELY WITH CAPTAIN MARVEL. THE STORIES ARE GOOD BUT THEY DON'T HAVE THAT SAME PUNCH AS WHEN THAT WHOLE THING WITH MR. MIND HAPPENED! IT'S NOT AS EXCITING!
HE'S ALWAYS EXCITING TO ME; I COULD WATCH HIM IN A BATHROBE EATING CORN FLAKES! ANY PLACE, ANYWHERE, ANY TIME...
MS. FIDELITY! COULD WE FOCUS HERE, PLEASE?
THAT WHOLE MR. MIND THING WAS RATINGS GOLD! NOW, THAT WAS A STORY! RATINGS WOULD SHOOT THROUGH THE ROOF IF SOMETHING BIG LIKE THAT WERE TO HAPPEN AGAIN...

"...BUT YOU NEVER KNOW WHEN A STORY LIKE THAT IS GOING TO BREAK!"

HEY DR. SIVANA, WHY HAVEN'T YOU DECORATED YOUR CELL YET? YOU SHOULD BE GETTING USED TO PRISON BY NOW.

YEAH! WHAT'S THE MATTER? NOT AS GOOD AS YOUR CUSHY DIGS WERE WHEN YOU WERE "ATTORNEY GENERAL OF THE UNITED STATES"?

BETTER GET USED TO IT; YOU'LL BE HERE FOR QUITE A AWHILE.

THAT'S WHAT YOU THINK!

DID YOU SAY SOMETHING, CONVICT?

OH, I MERELY SAID THAT I NEED A TISSUE TO WIPE MY GLASSES WITH... PLEASE.

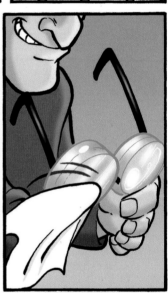

TCK

BBZZZT BBZZZT

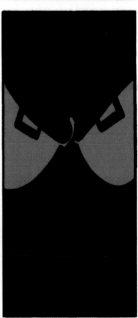

11

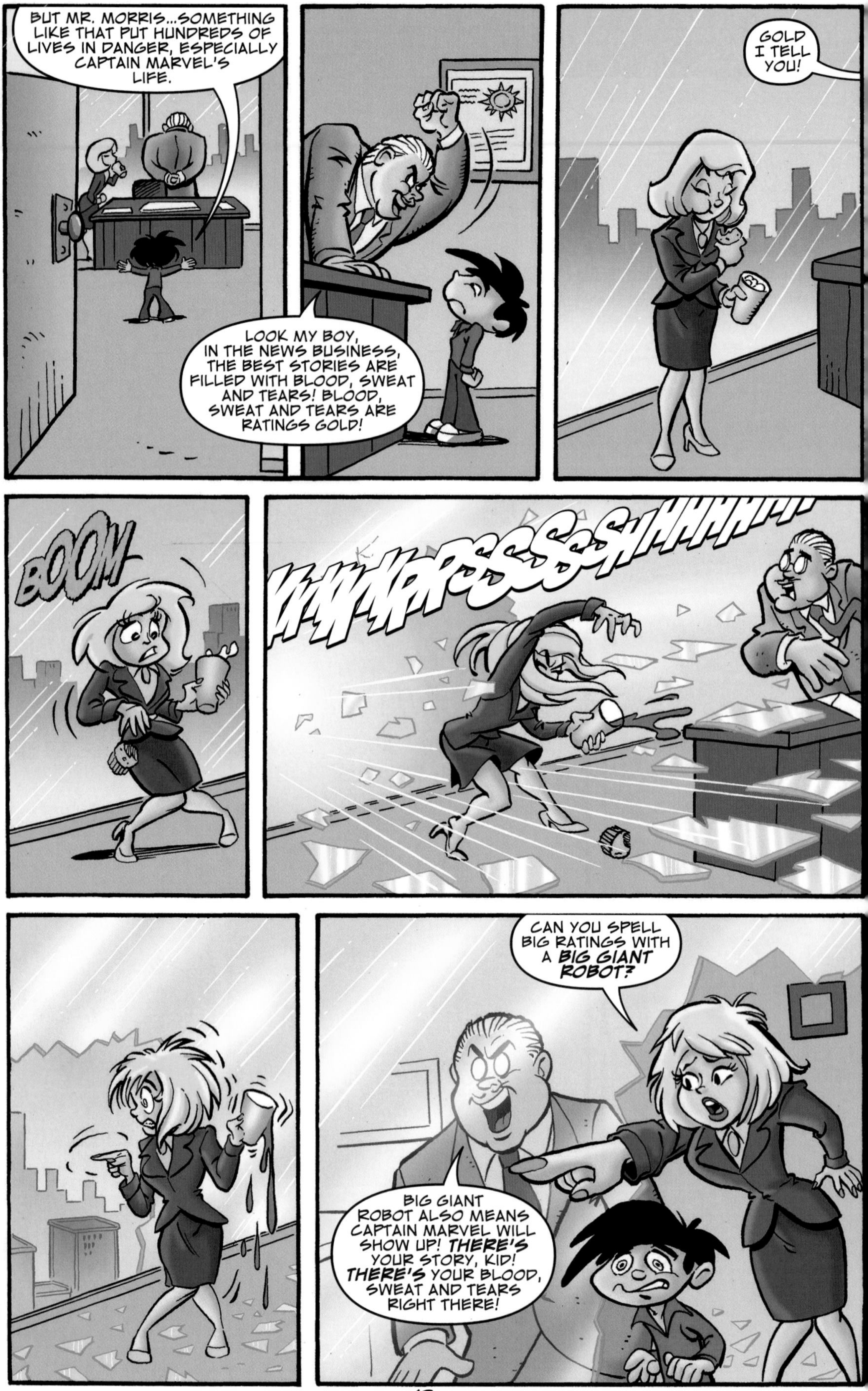
BUT MR. MORRIS...SOMETHING LIKE THAT PUT HUNDREDS OF LIVES IN DANGER, ESPECIALLY CAPTAIN MARVEL'S LIFE.
LOOK MY BOY, IN THE NEWS BUSINESS, THE BEST STORIES ARE FILLED WITH BLOOD, SWEAT AND TEARS! BLOOD, SWEAT AND TEARS ARE RATINGS GOLD!
GOLD I TELL YOU!
BOOM
KKKKKRRRSSSSSHHHHHH
CAN YOU SPELL BIG RATINGS WITH A **BIG GIANT ROBOT?**
BIG GIANT ROBOT ALSO MEANS CAPTAIN MARVEL WILL SHOW UP! **THERE'S** YOUR STORY, KID! **THERE'S** YOUR BLOOD, SWEAT AND TEARS RIGHT THERE!

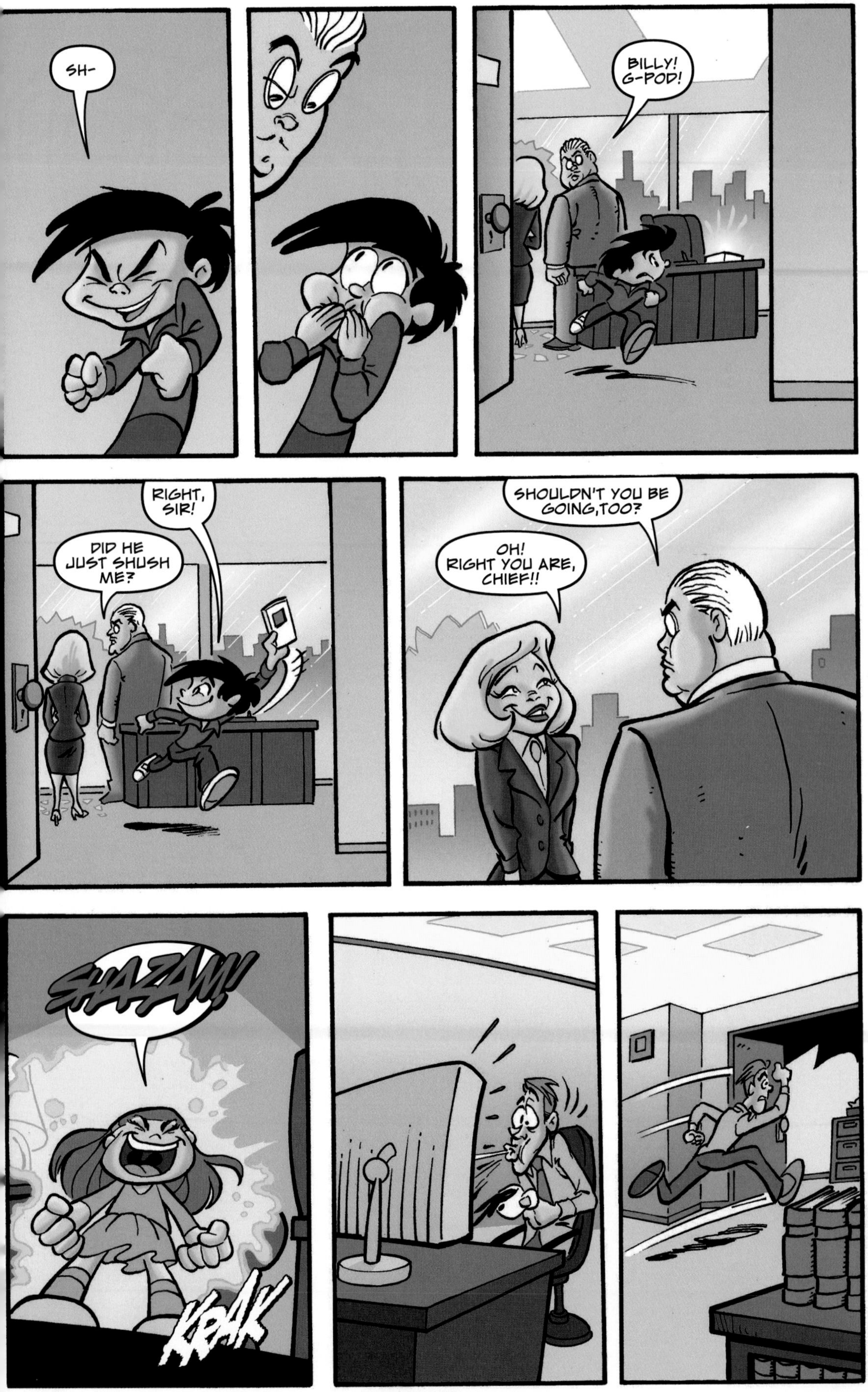
SH-
BILLY! G-POD!
DID HE JUST SHUSH ME?
RIGHT, SIR!
SHOULDN'T YOU BE GOING,TOO?
OH! RIGHT YOU ARE, CHIEF!!
SHAZAM!
KRAK

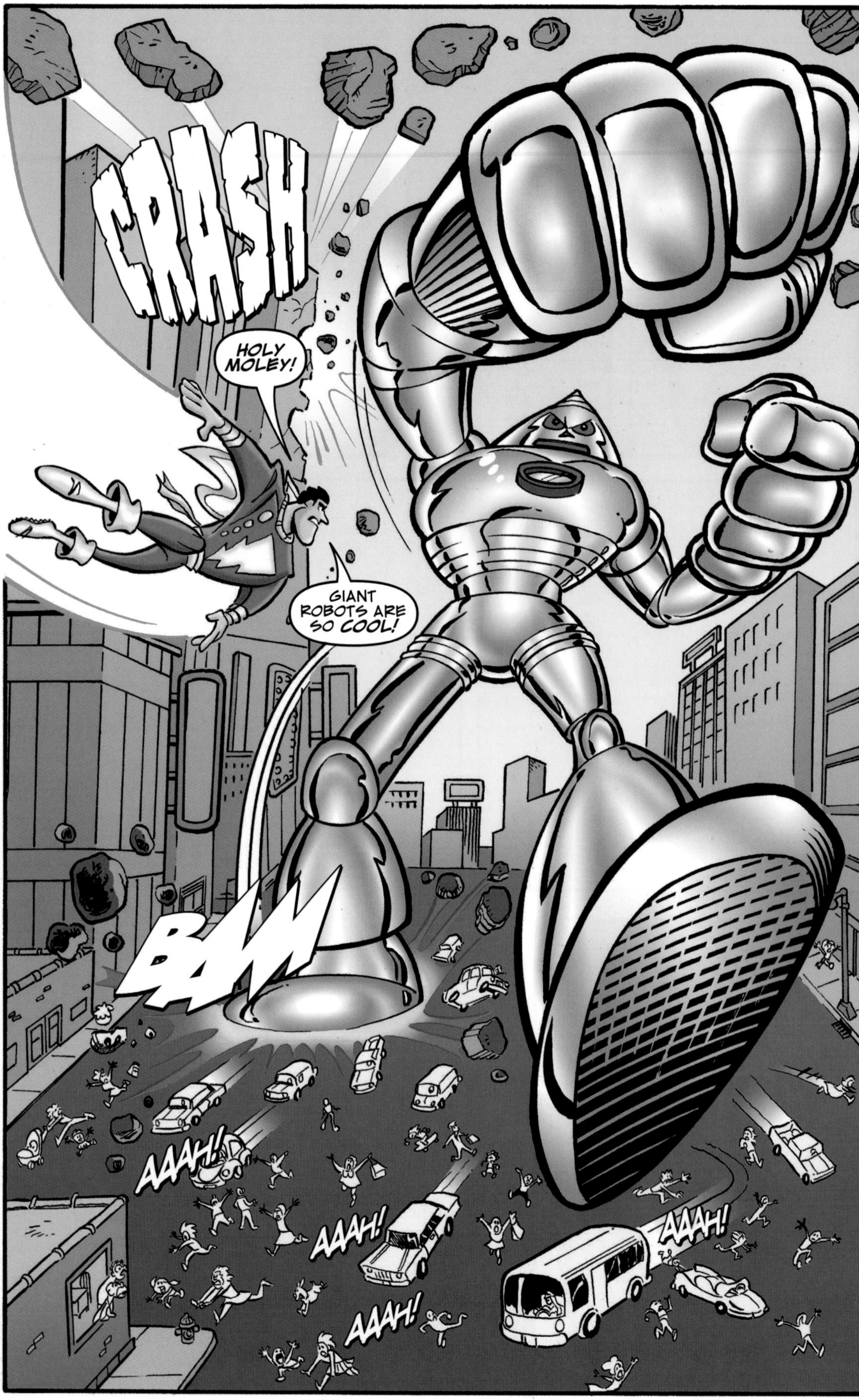
CRASH
HOLY MOLEY!
GIANT ROBOTS ARE SO COOL!
BAM
AAAH!
AAAH!
AAAH!
AAAH!

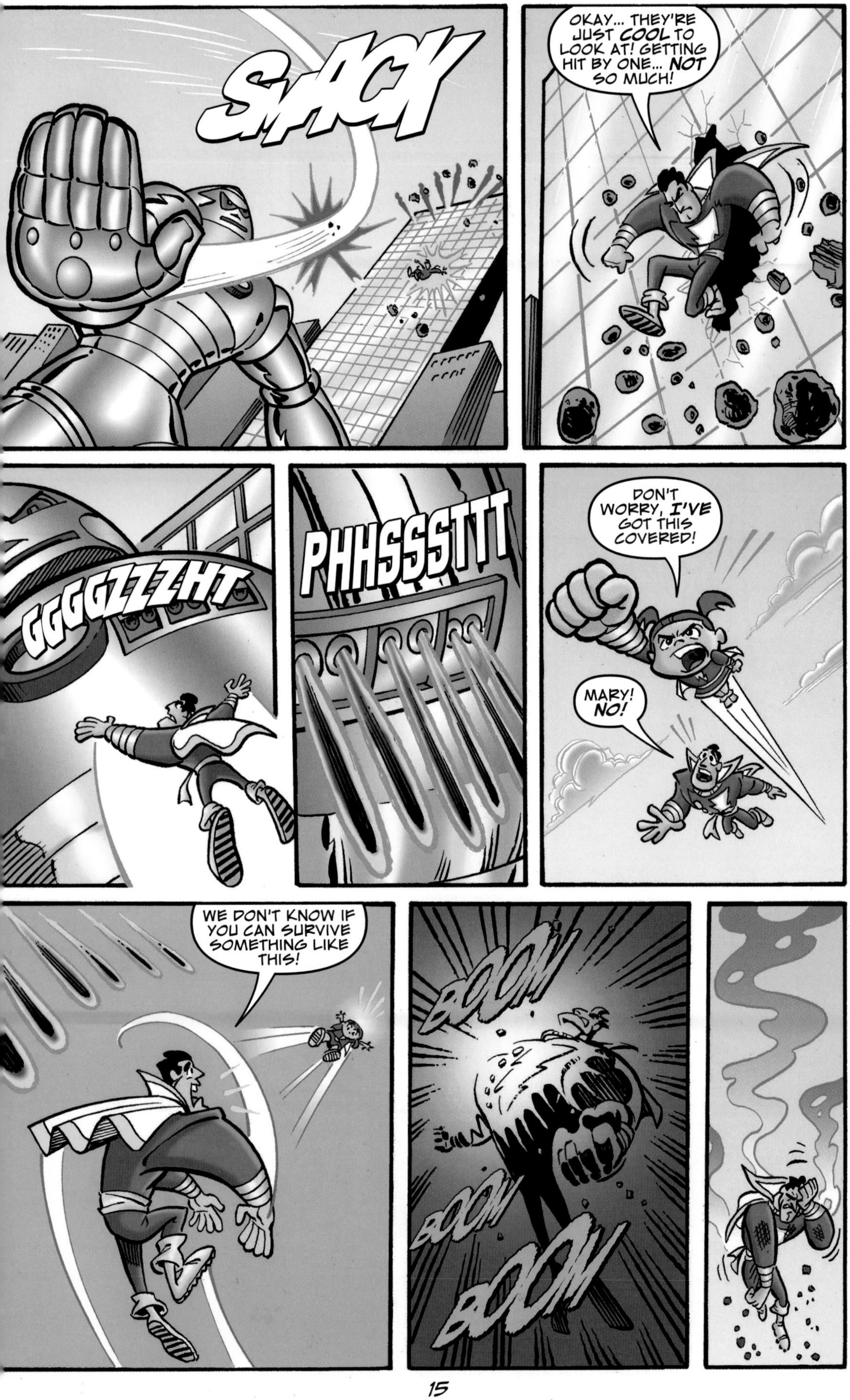
SMACK
OKAY... THEY'RE JUST COOL TO LOOK AT! GETTING HIT BY ONE... NOT SO MUCH!
GGGGZZZZHT
PHHSSSTTT
DON'T WORRY, I'VE GOT THIS COVERED!
MARY! NO!
WE DON'T KNOW IF YOU CAN SURVIVE SOMETHING LIKE THIS!
BOOM
BOOM
BOOM

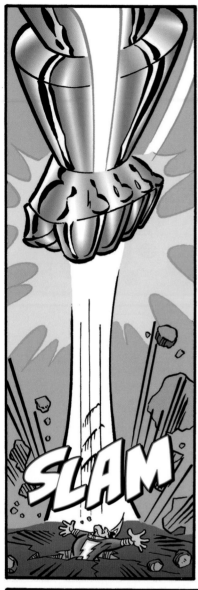

SLAM

KABOOOF

RUMMMBLE

CRACK

OH MY GOSH!
OH MY GOSH!
OH MY GOSH!

ARE YOU
OKAY?

LOOK
OUT!!!

SLAM

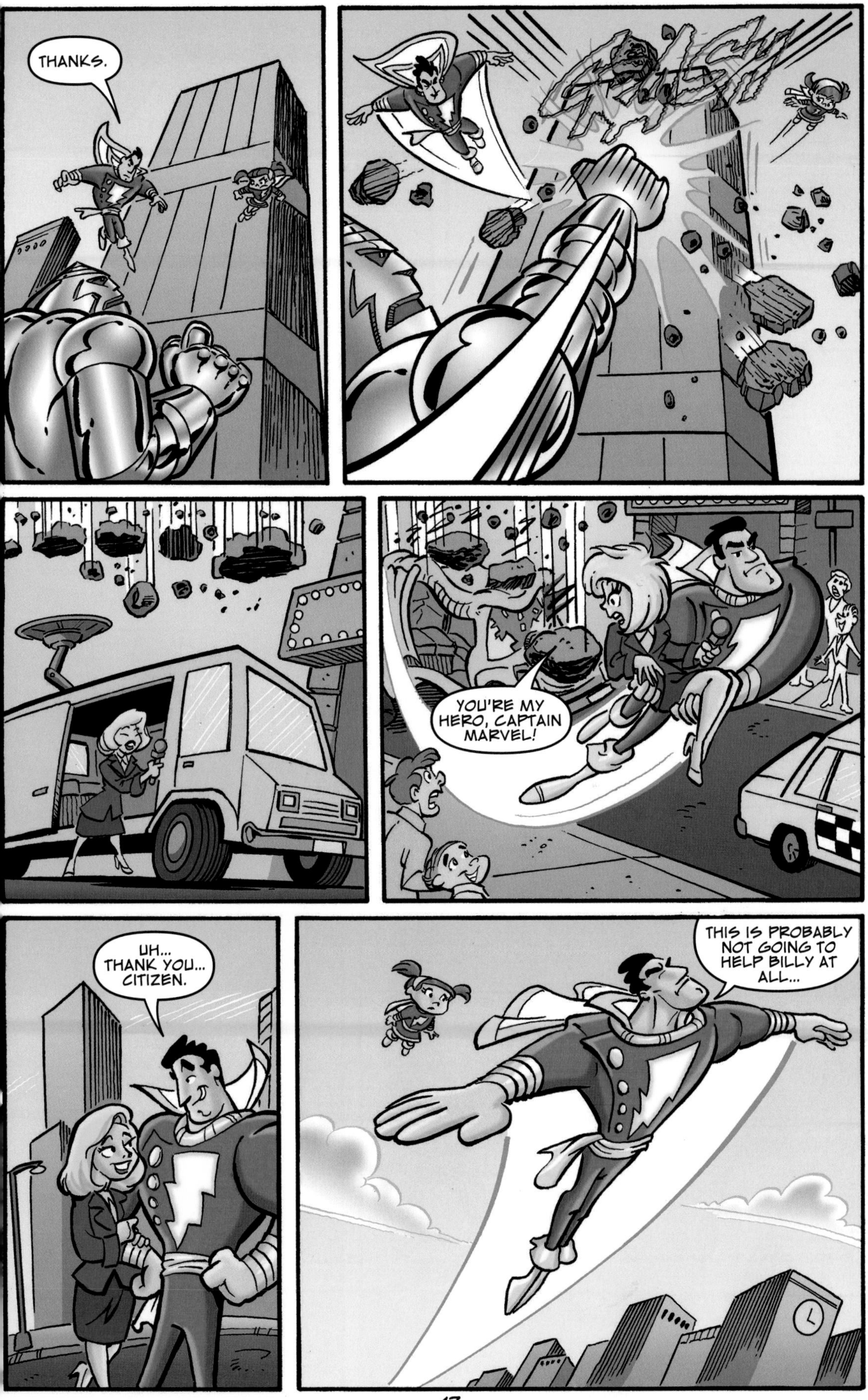
THANKS.
YOU'RE MY HERO, CAPTAIN MARVEL!
UH... THANK YOU... CITIZEN.
THIS IS PROBABLY NOT GOING TO HELP BILLY AT ALL...

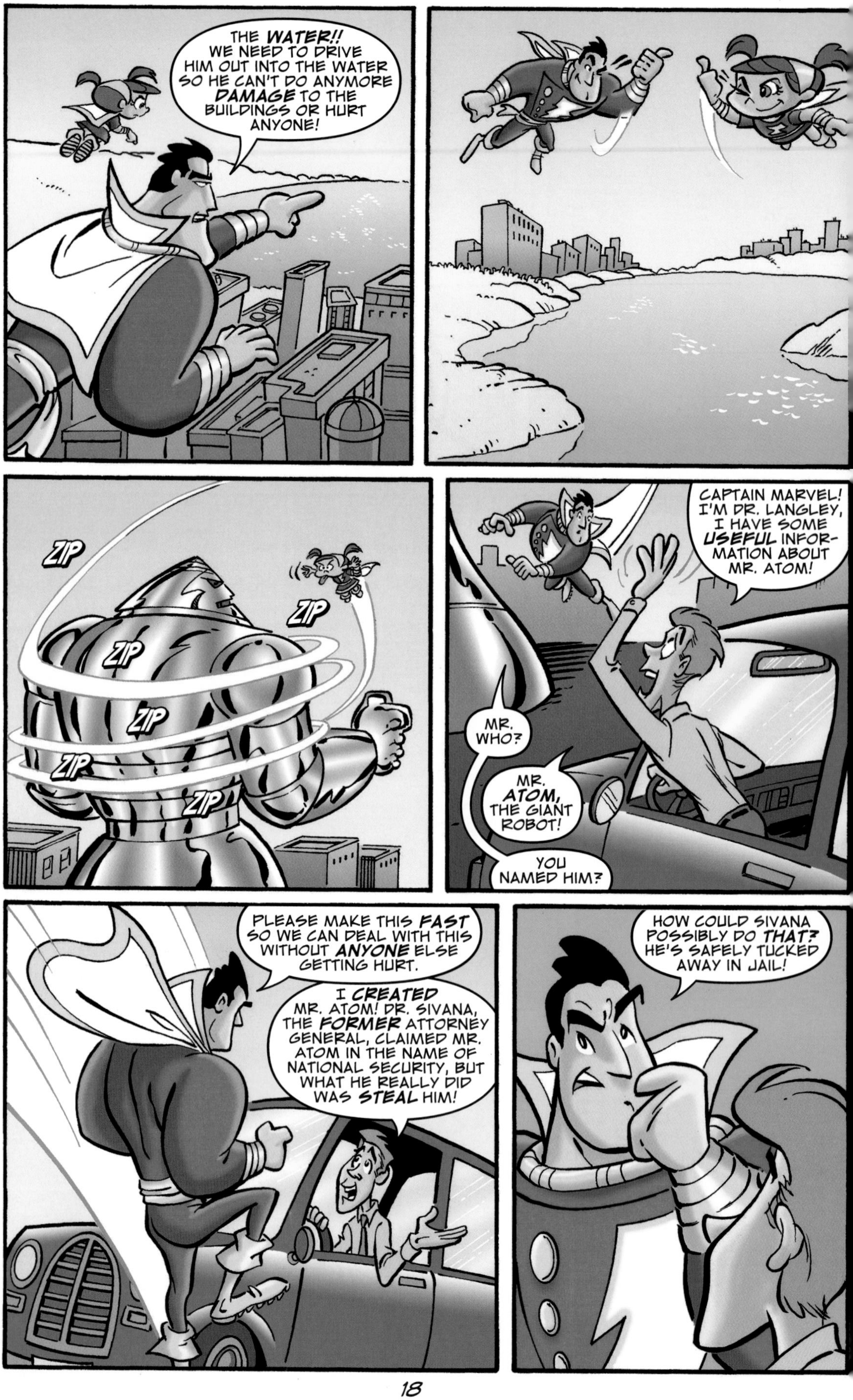
THE WATER!! WE NEED TO DRIVE HIM OUT INTO THE WATER SO HE CAN'T DO ANYMORE DAMAGE TO THE BUILDINGS OR HURT ANYONE!
ZIP
ZIP
ZIP
ZIP
ZIP
ZIP
CAPTAIN MARVEL! I'M DR. LANGLEY, I HAVE SOME USEFUL INFORMATION ABOUT MR. ATOM!
MR. WHO?
MR. ATOM, THE GIANT ROBOT!
YOU NAMED HIM?
PLEASE MAKE THIS FAST SO WE CAN DEAL WITH THIS WITHOUT ANYONE ELSE GETTING HURT.
I CREATED MR. ATOM! DR. SIVANA, THE FORMER ATTORNEY GENERAL, CLAIMED MR. ATOM IN THE NAME OF NATIONAL SECURITY, BUT WHAT HE REALLY DID WAS STEAL HIM!
HOW COULD SIVANA POSSIBLY DO THAT? HE'S SAFELY TUCKED AWAY IN JAIL!

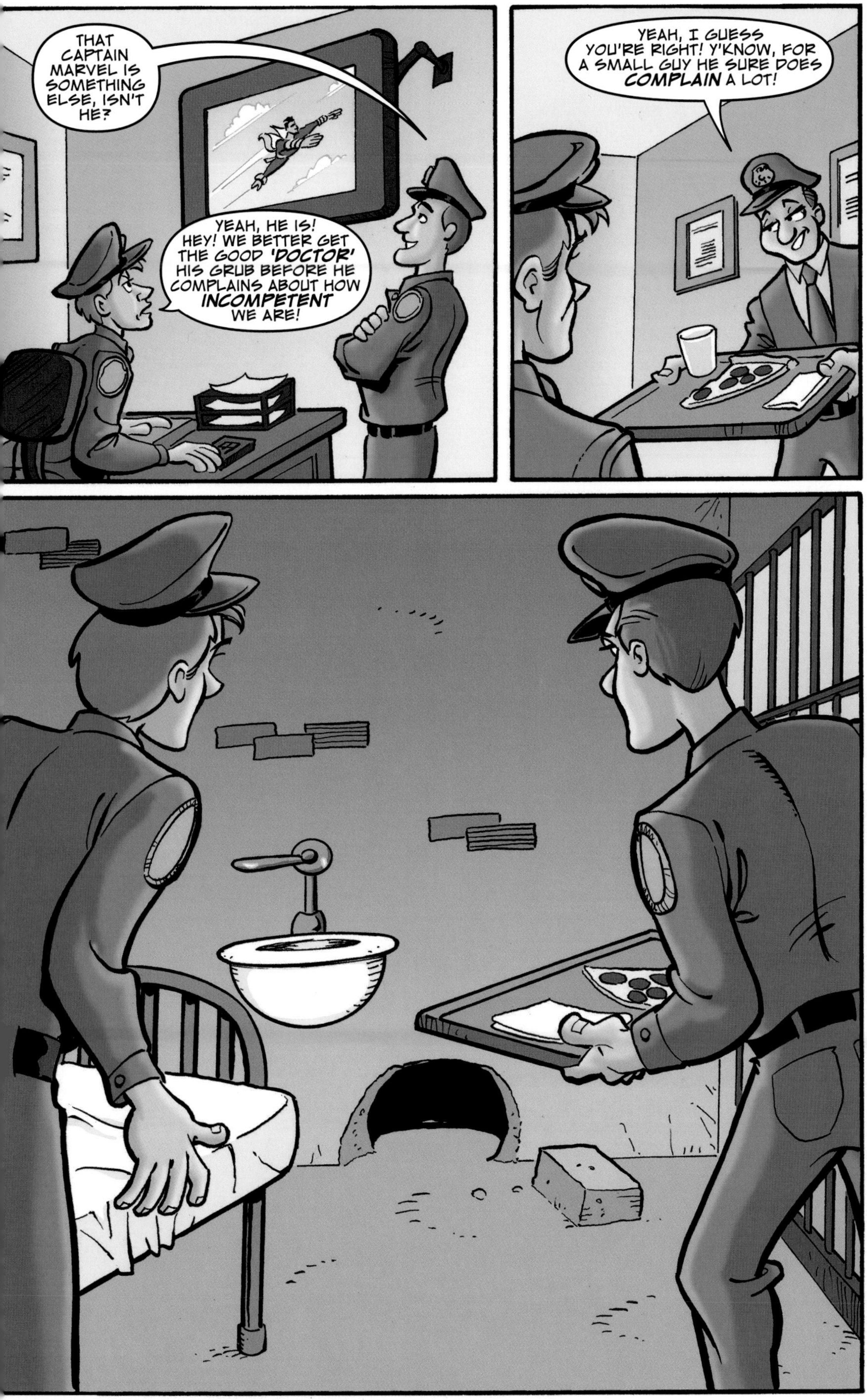

THAT CAPTAIN MARVEL IS SOMETHING ELSE, ISN'T HE?
YEAH, HE IS! HEY! WE BETTER GET THE GOOD 'DOCTOR' HIS GRUB BEFORE HE COMPLAINS ABOUT HOW INCOMPETENT WE ARE!
YEAH, I GUESS YOU'RE RIGHT! Y'KNOW, FOR A SMALL GUY HE SURE DOES COMPLAIN A LOT!

SIVANA **CONFISCATED** MR. ATOM AS WELL AS PLANS FOR **SEVERAL** OTHER INVENTIONS OF MINE TO EVENTUALLY **SELL** AS WAR MACHINES, I FEAR! I'VE BEEN **TRYING** TO CUT THROUGH RED TAPE FOR YEARS, TRYING TO GET BACK ALL OF MY WORK.

SORRY TO INTERRUPT YOUR CONVERSATION...

...BUT I **COULD** USE A LITTLE HELP HERE!

WAIT! THERE'S A WAY TO **DEACTIVATE** HIM!

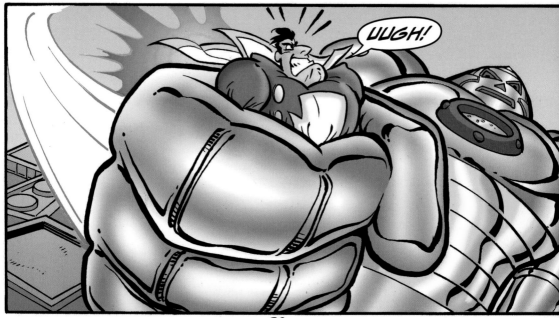

UUGH!

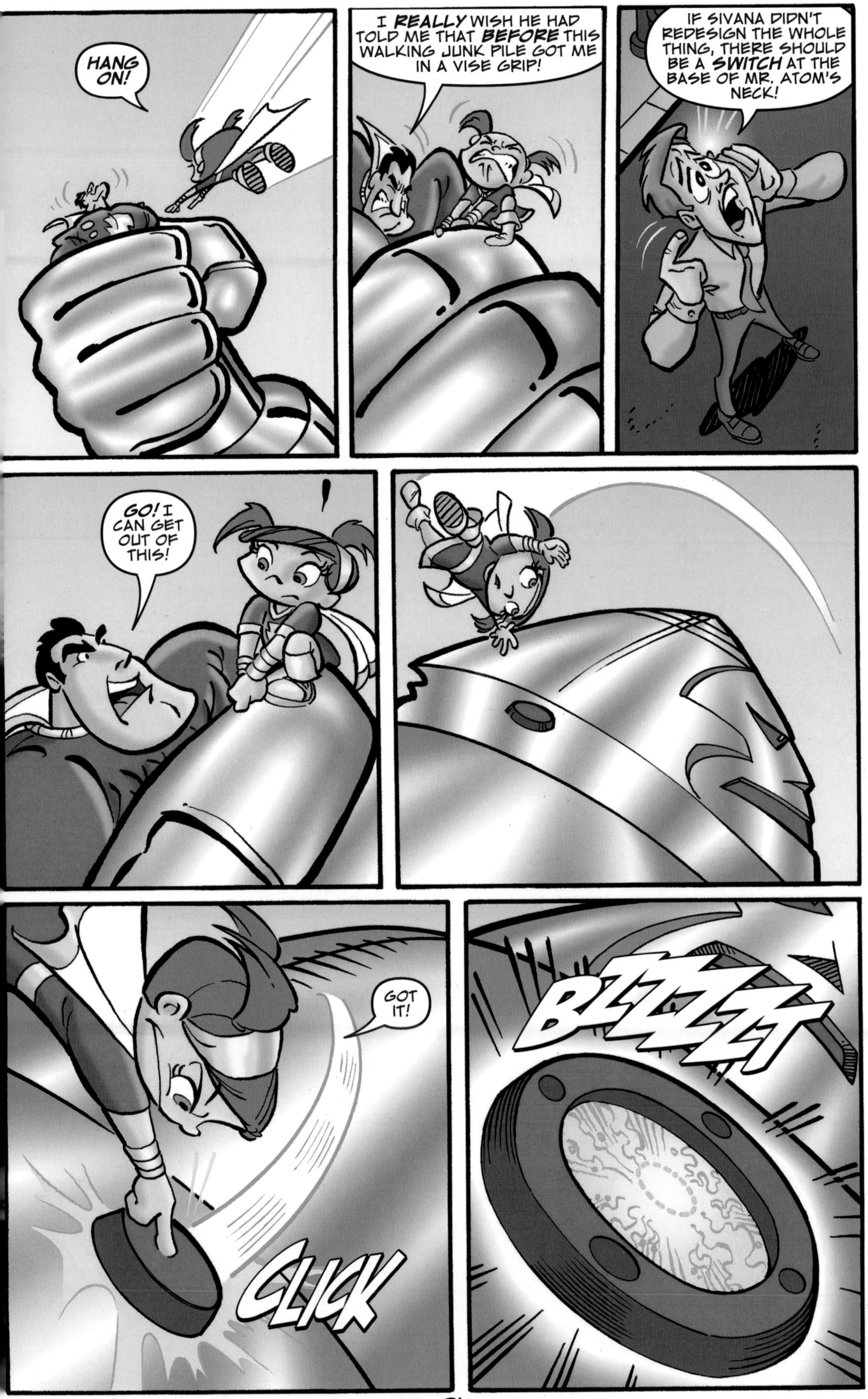
HANG ON!
I REALLY WISH HE HAD TOLD ME THAT BEFORE THIS WALKING JUNK PILE GOT ME IN A VISE GRIP!
IF SIVANA DIDN'T REDESIGN THE WHOLE THING, THERE SHOULD BE A SWITCH AT THE BASE OF MR. ATOM'S NECK!
GO! I CAN GET OUT OF THIS!
GOT IT!
CLICK
BIZZZT

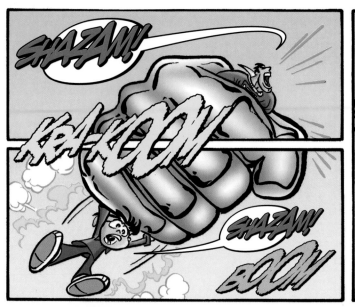

SHAZAM!

KRA-BOOM

SHAZAM! BOOM

OKAY, "MR. ATOM," YOU'RE TOAST!

NO!

KACRUNKH

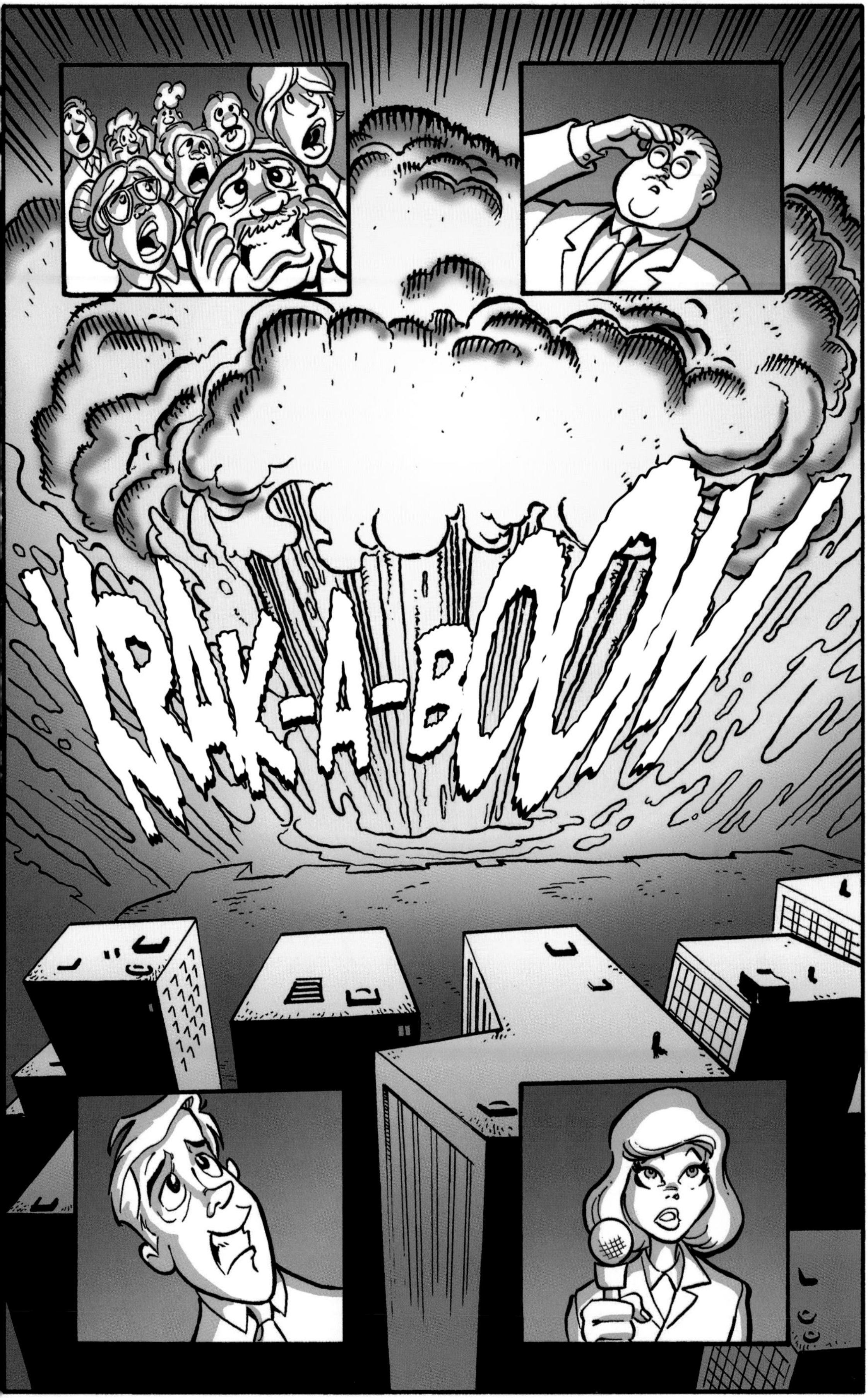
KRAK-A-BOOM

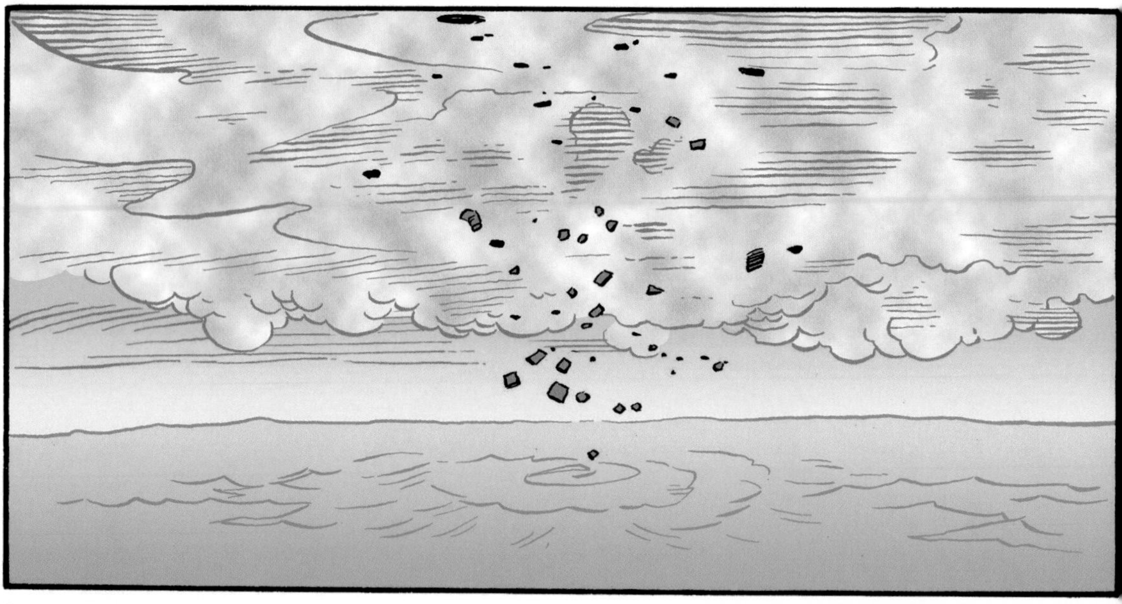

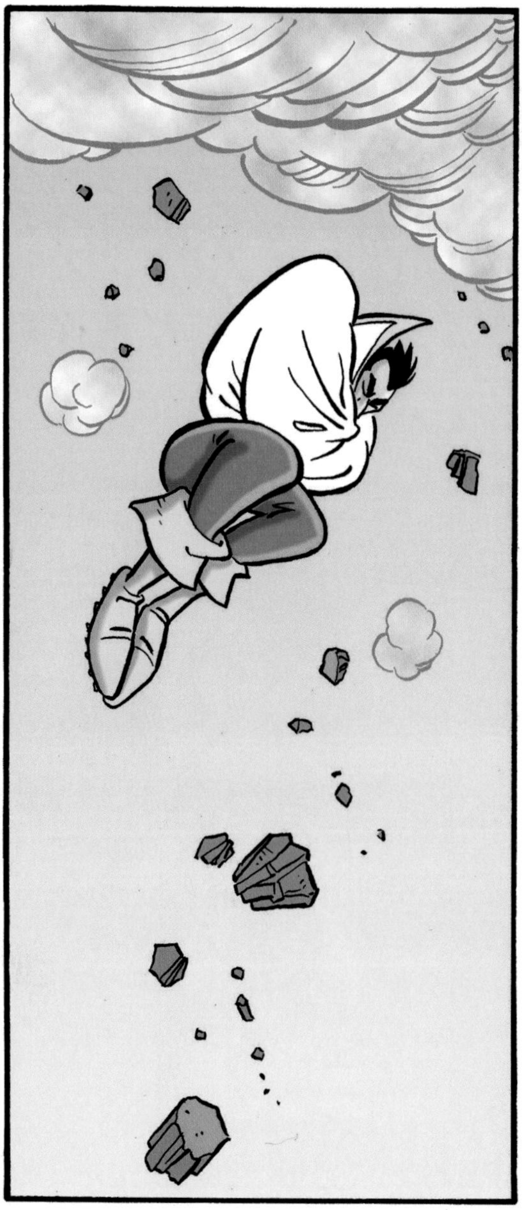

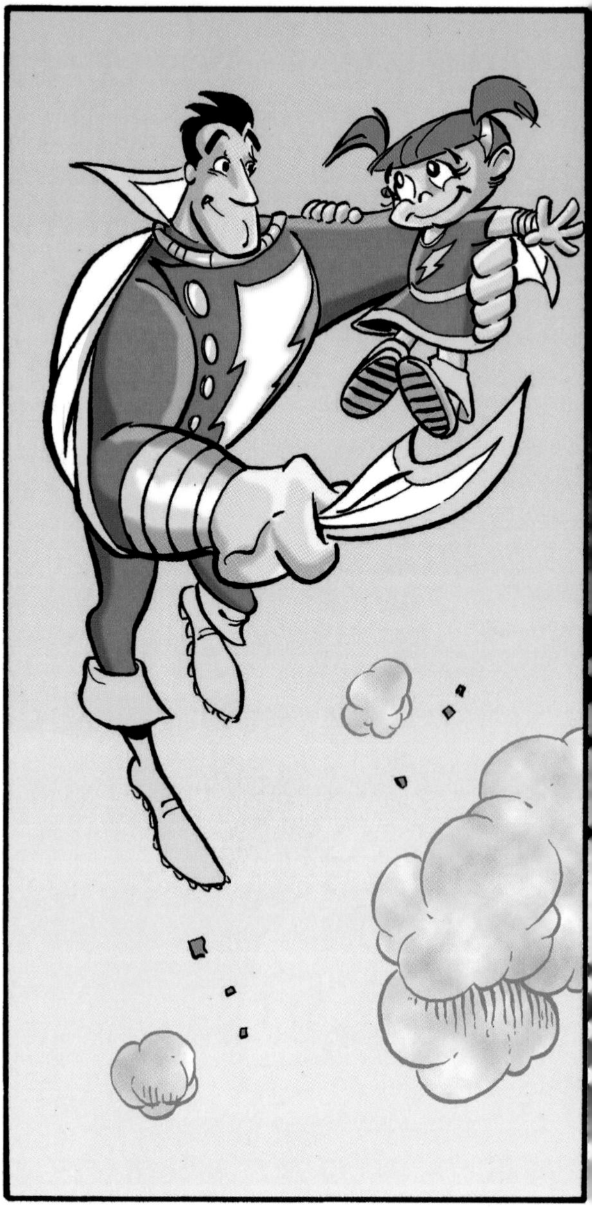

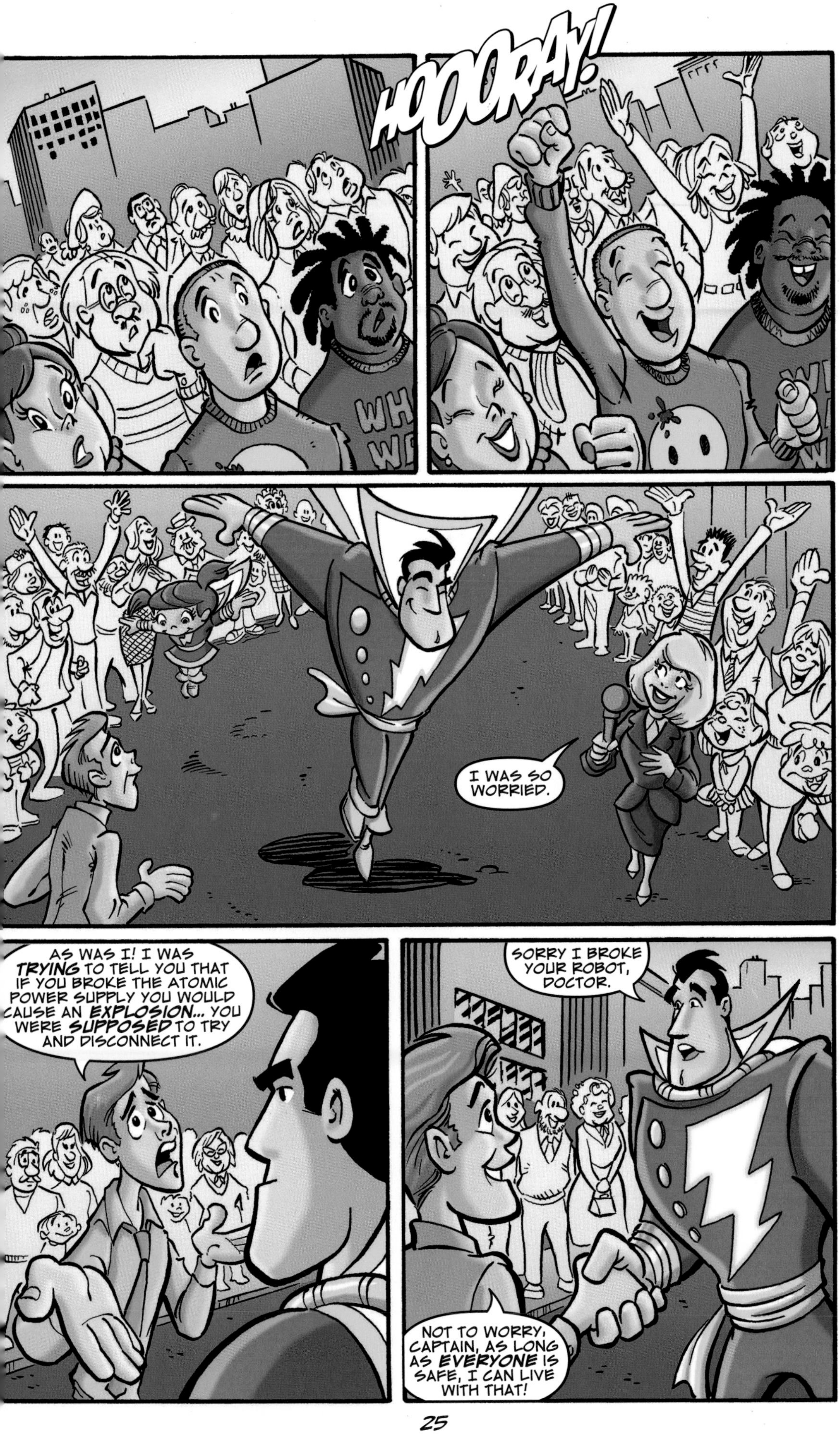
HOOORAY!
I WAS SO WORRIED.
AS WAS I! I WAS TRYING TO TELL YOU THAT IF YOU BROKE THE ATOMIC POWER SUPPLY YOU WOULD CAUSE AN EXPLOSION... YOU WERE SUPPOSED TO TRY AND DISCONNECT IT.
SORRY I BROKE YOUR ROBOT, DOCTOR.
NOT TO WORRY, CAPTAIN, AS LONG AS EVERYONE IS SAFE, I CAN LIVE WITH THAT!

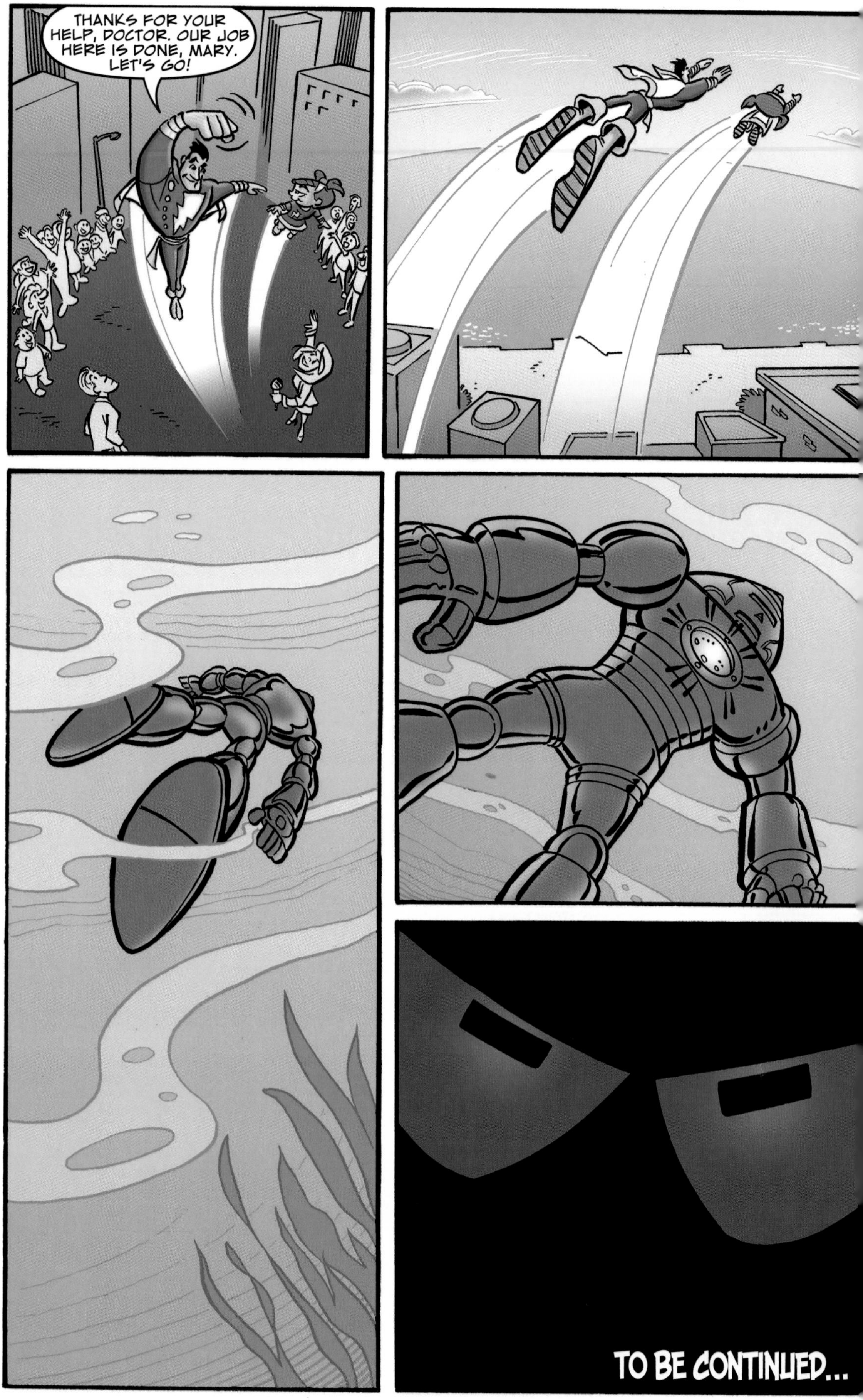
THANKS FOR YOUR HELP, DOCTOR. OUR JOB HERE IS DONE, MARY. LET'S GO!
TO BE CONTINUED...

CREATORS

ART BALTAZAR – CO-WRITER

Born in Chicago, **Art Baltazar** has been cartooning ever since he can recall. Art has worked on award-winning series like Tiny Titans and Superman Family Adventures. He lives outside of Chicago with his wife, Rose, and children Sonny, Gordon, and Audrey.

FRANCO – CO-WRITER

Franco Aureliani has been drawing comics ever since he could hold a crayon. He resides in upstate New York with his wife, Ivette, and son, Nicolas, and spends most of his days working on comics. Franco has worked on Superman Family Adventures and Tiny Titans, and he also teaches high school art.

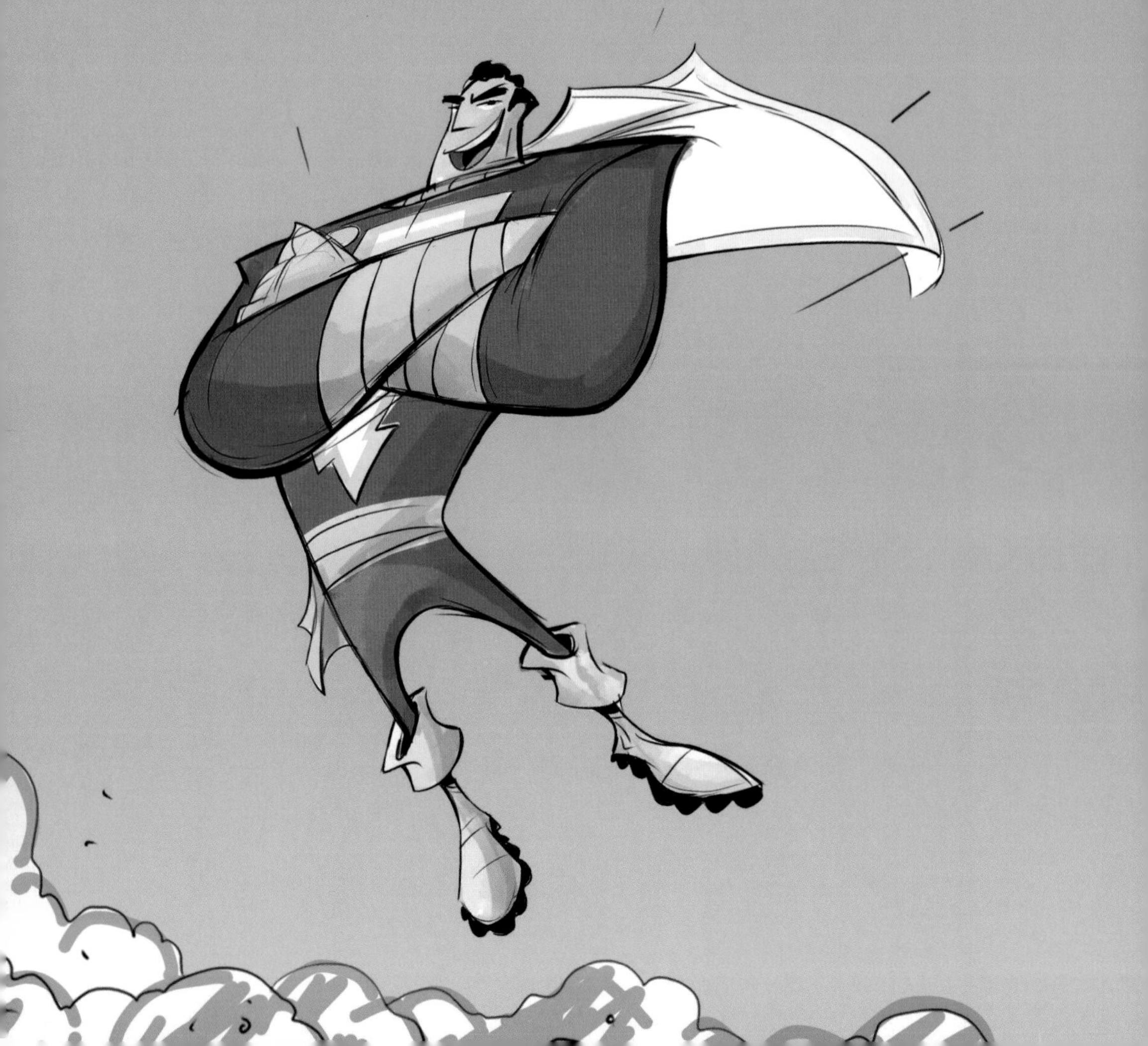

GLOSSARY

atomic (uh-TOM-ik)--of, relating to, or using the incredible energy that is produced when atoms are split apart

citizen (SIT-uh-zuhn)--a person who legally belongs to a country and has the rights and protection of that country

confiscated (KON-fuh-skay-tid)--took something away from someone, especially as punishment or to enforce the law or rules

convict (KON-vikt)--a person who has been found guilty of a crime and sent to prison. A prisoner.

cushy (KOOSH-ee)--very easy and pleasant

deactivate (dee-AK-tuh-vayt)--to make something no longer active or effective

decorated (DEK-uh-ray-tid)--made something more attractive by putting something on it

exclusive (ik-SKLOO-siv)--available to only one person or group. An exclusive is also a piece of news obtained by a news organization along with the right to use it before anyone else.

footage (FOOT-ij)--scenes or action recorded on film or video

incompetent (in-KOM-puh-tuhnt)--lacking necessary ability or skills

latte (LAH-tay)--hot espresso (a strong type of coffee) made with steamed milk that is usually topped with foamed milk

VISUAL QUESTIONS & PROMPTS

1. Billy has to balance his life as a normal kid with his secret identity as a grown-up super hero. What kind of problems does Billy face in this book?

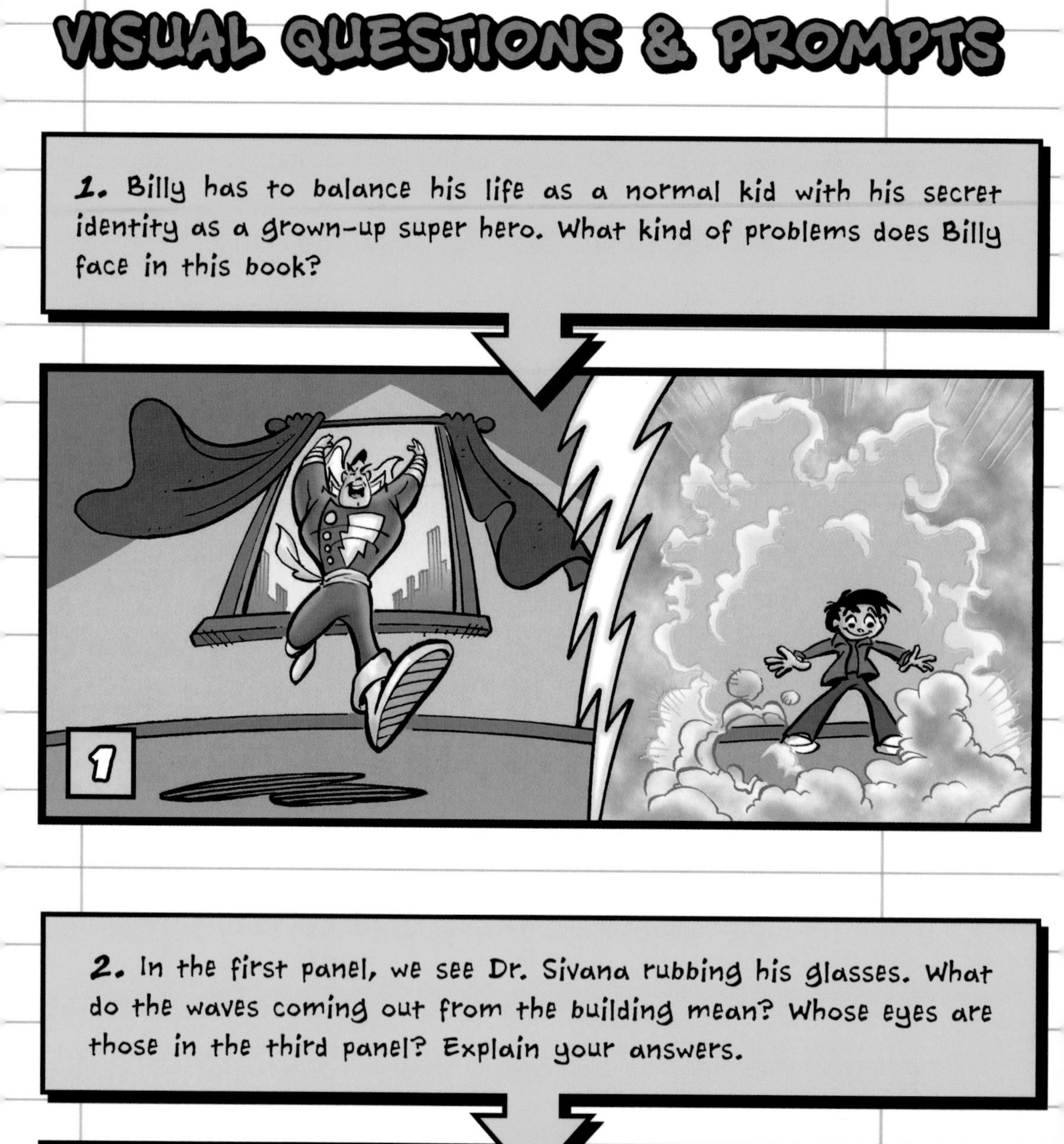
1

2. In the first panel, we see Dr. Sivana rubbing his glasses. What do the waves coming out from the building mean? Whose eyes are those in the third panel? Explain your answers.

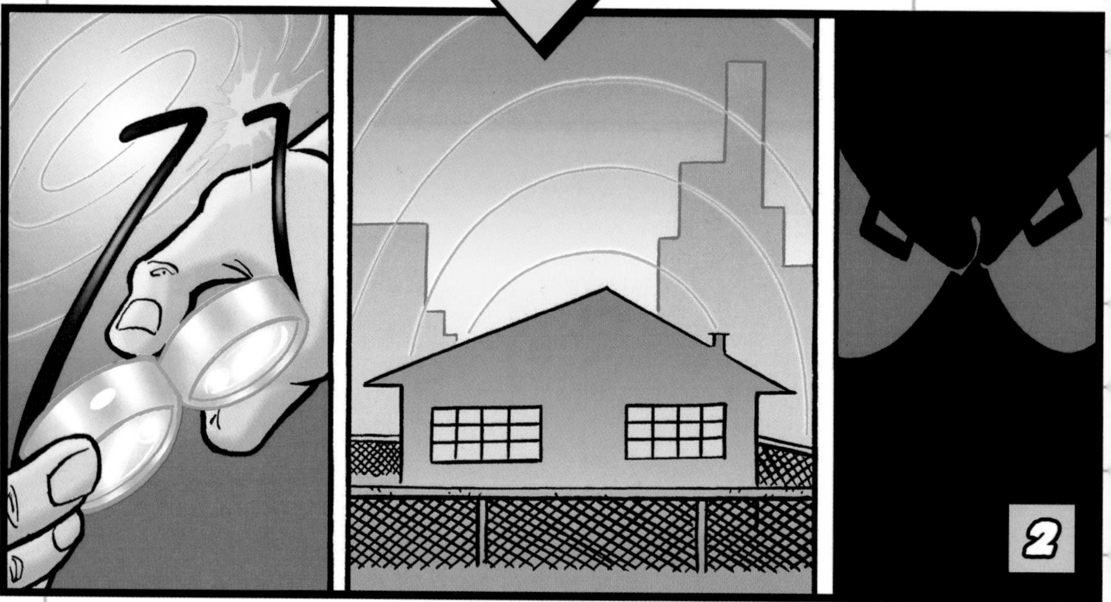
2

3. What is happening in these two panels? Why did Captain Marvel do what he did, and why was it a good thing?

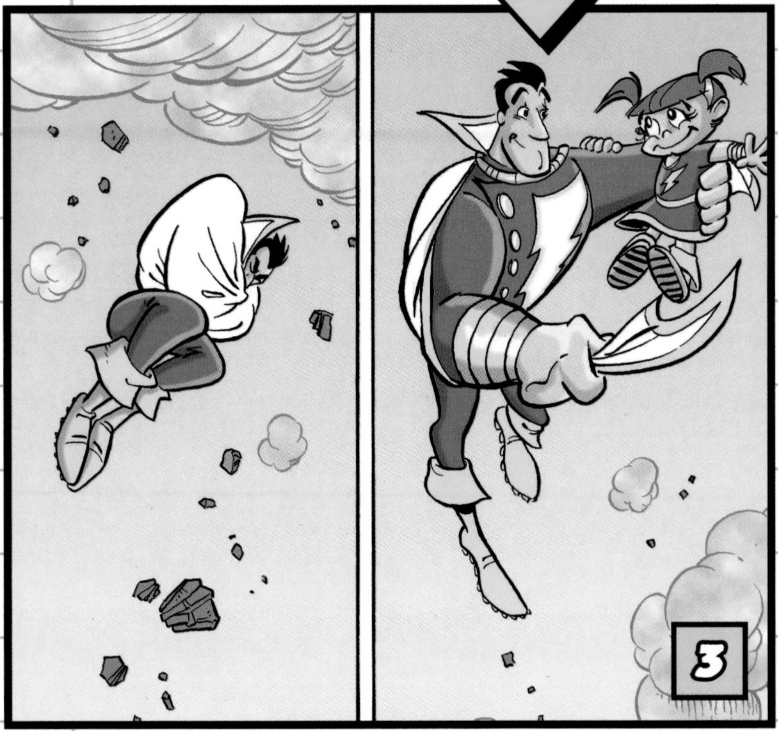
3

4. How do you think Sivana escaped his cell? What evidence do you have?

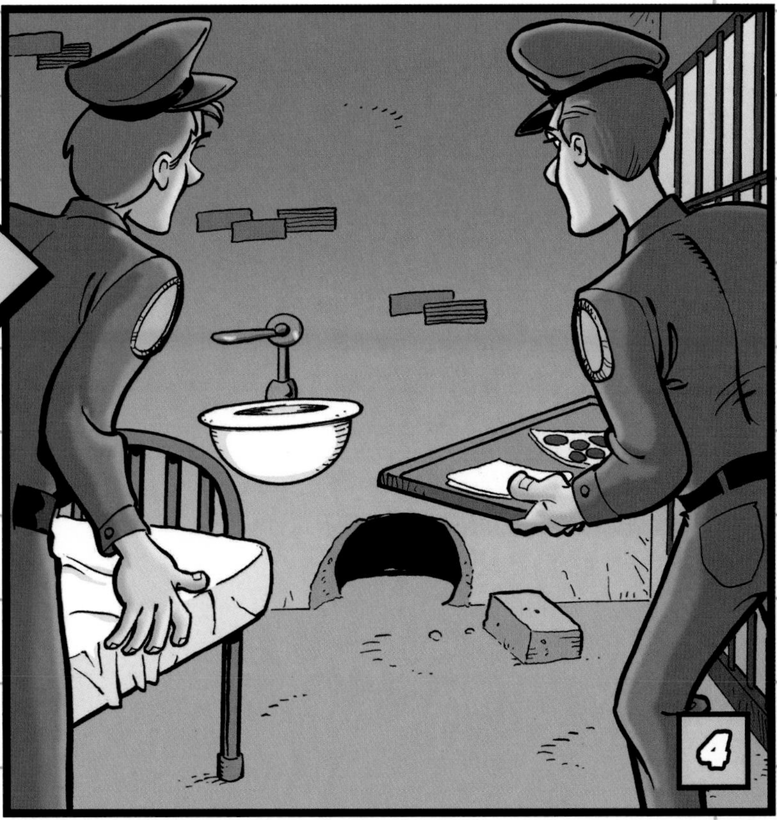
4

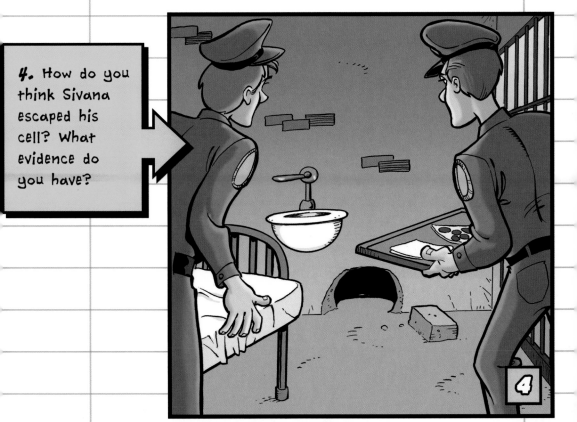

READ THEM ALL!

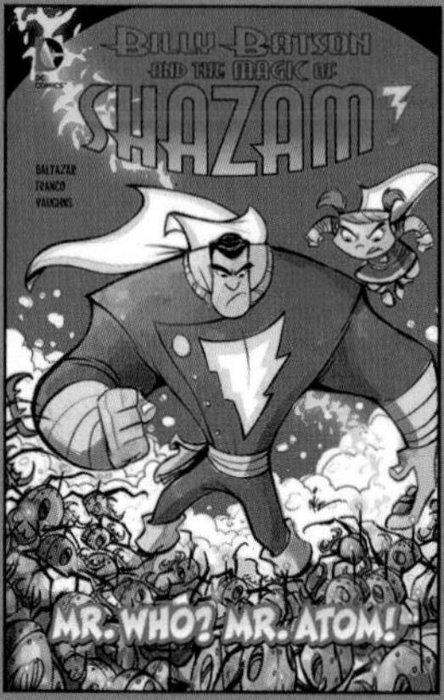
BILLY BATSON AND THE MAGIC OF SHAZAM!
BALTAZAR
FRANCO
VAUGHNS
MR. WHO? MR. ATOM!

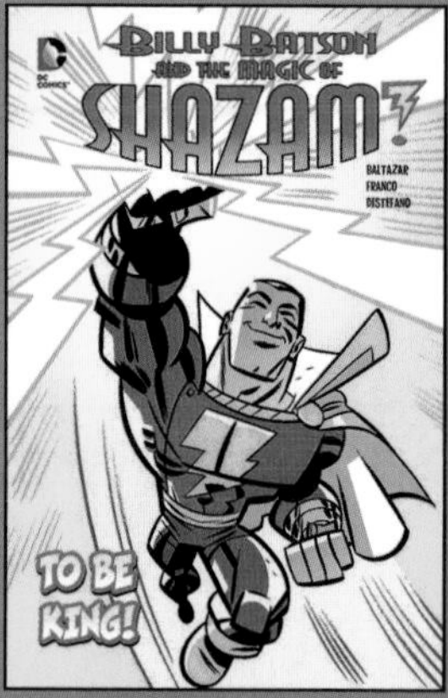
BILLY BATSON AND THE MAGIC OF SHAZAM!
BALTAZAR
FRANCO
DISTEFANO
TO BE KING!

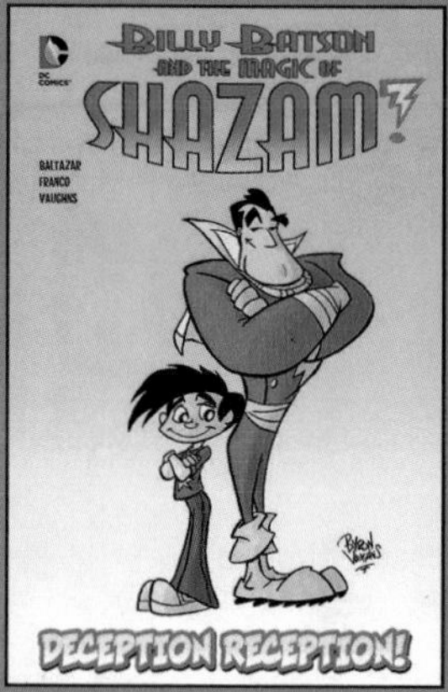
BILLY BATSON AND THE MAGIC OF SHAZAM!
BALTAZAR
FRANCO
VAUGHNS
DECEPTION RECEPTION!

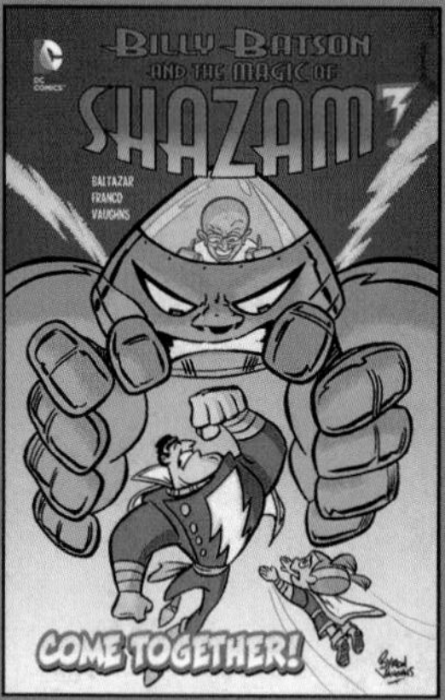
BILLY BATSON AND THE MAGIC OF SHAZAM!
BALTAZAR
FRANCO
VAUGHNS
COME TOGETHER!

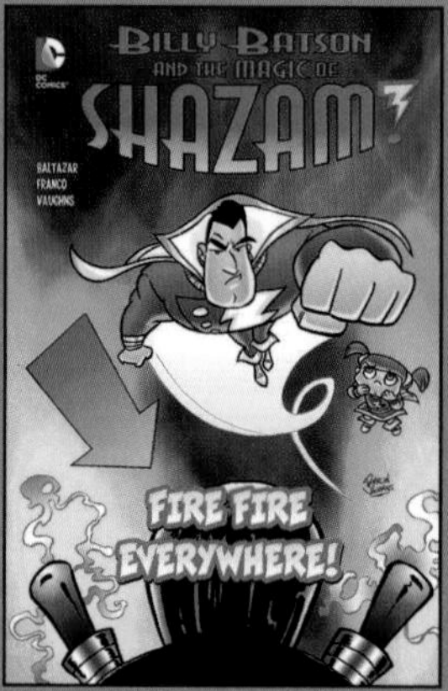
BILLY BATSON AND THE MAGIC OF SHAZAM!
BALTAZAR
FRANCO
VAUGHNS
FIRE FIRE EVERYWHERE!

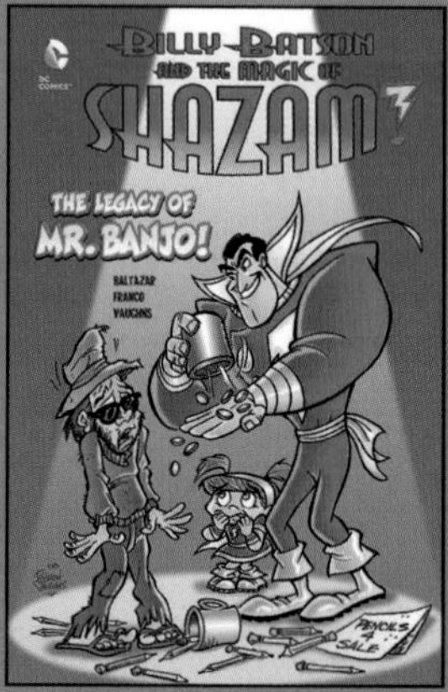
BILLY BATSON AND THE MAGIC OF SHAZAM!
THE LEGACY OF MR. BANJO!
BALTAZAR
FRANCO
VAUGHNS

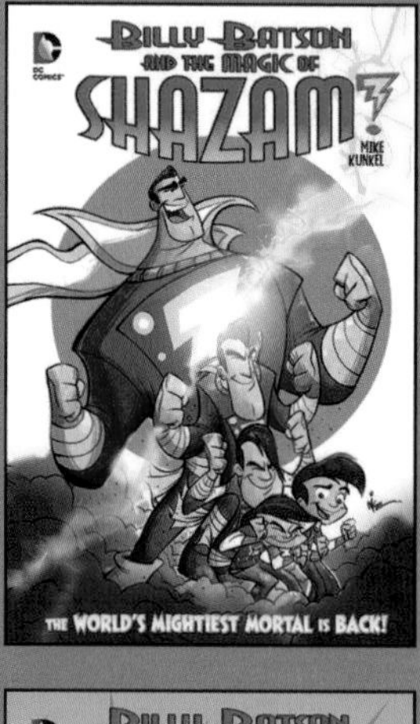
BILLY BATSON AND THE MAGIC OF SHAZAM!
MIKE KUNKEL
THE WORLD'S MIGHTIEST MORTAL IS BACK!

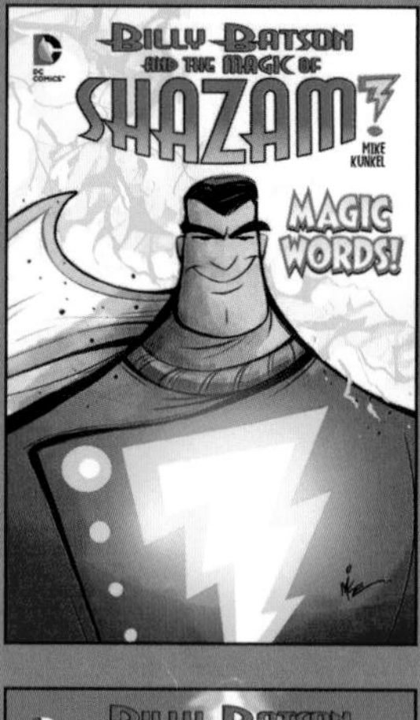
BILLY BATSON AND THE MAGIC OF SHAZAM!
MIKE KUNKEL
MAGIC WORDS!

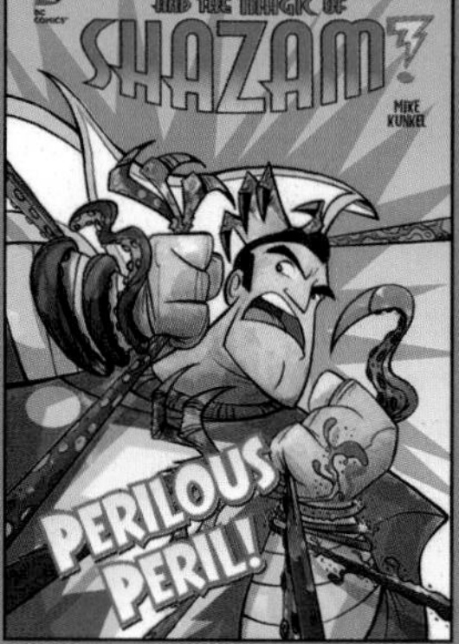
BILLY BATSON AND THE MAGIC OF SHAZAM!
MIKE KUNKEL
PERILOUS PERIL!

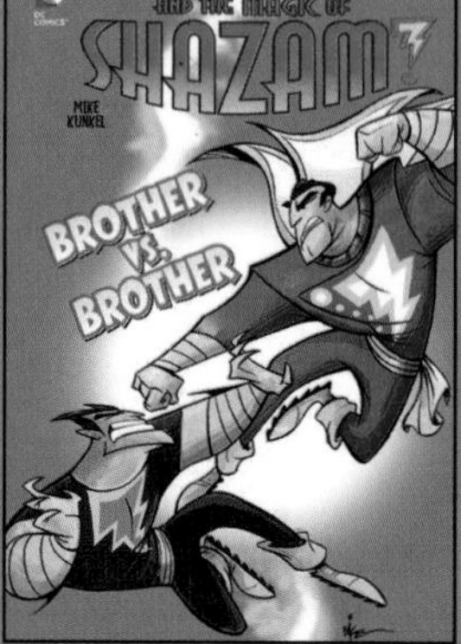
BILLY BATSON AND THE MAGIC OF SHAZAM!
MIKE KUNKEL
BROTHER VS. BROTHER